The

ISBN 978-1-7333177-0-2

Written by John Opalenik
Cover art by Amanda Carlone
Edited by Nancy Manning

Printed in The United States of America

opalenikj@gmail.com

Visit www.johnopalenik.com

Dedicated to Amanda for her love and support, to Marc for his enthusiasm, to Nancy for her keen eye and faith in me, and most of all to you, dear reader.

1

"It's heavy!" The boy complained as he held up the sturdy .308 bolt action rifle, which seemed completely out of place in his grandmother's kitchen. He ran one hand through his curly hair and wiped his sweaty palms on his pants.

"It's got to be, otherwise the kickback will knock it out of your hands." His father hefted his own rifle in his arms and adjusted the collar of his dark green jacket with the bare minimum reflective orange patches, designed to signal fellow hunters not to shoot him.

"I just don't know why we have to go on Sunday. Sundays we're supposed to have dinner with Grandma."

"Listen, Fran. I hunted in these woods when I was your age, and now it's your turn. This is a big day for you. Don't whine about becoming a man. I wish my old man took me on a trip like this." Fran's father never missed an opportunity to remind him that he would always be a better father than his father had been, simply because he stuck around past Fran's third birthday, which is more than his grandfather had done for his son. He'd made it a point of doing all of the things that he'd wished his dad had done with him, such as hunting and fishing. Things that he thought would help turn his boy into a man. "Tonight, the girls are going to eat some takeout, and we're going to eat our kill tonight."

"I don't know if I could ever shoot a cute little bunny." Fran frowned, knowing that his protests would go unheard.

"Then you better hope we find something bigger." His father grinned and piled his son into his old pickup truck. They drove slowly down the dirt road that led half a mile into the deep forest across the street from Fran's grandmother's house.

They got out of the truck and the man checked his camouflage backpack one last time to make sure he had everything he needed. "Do you have your knife?"

Fran gestured to the folding knife tucked into his front pocket to let his father know that he'd followed directions and come prepared. "What if we don't find anything?"

"Francisco Rivera." Fran's father only used his son's full name when he needed to make Fran know he was being serious. "From here on, we're silent. Follow what I do, and look for my signals. Now follow me."

The rifle felt heavy in his arms. After countless afternoons in the woods playing army, using a stick as his weapon, the real thing almost felt wrong. This seemed so much more serious than carefree afternoons playing at being a soldier with his friends Jack and Charlie, with Jack's younger brother, Brad sometimes trailing behind. Fran struggled to keep up with his father while simultaneously following his order to remain perfectly quiet. When his father dropped to one knee and shouldered his rifle, Fran mimicked his movements instinctively. He looked up at his father before bringing his gaze down to his left knee which he'd pressed into the muddy ground.

The man wrapped his arm around the boy's throat and extended his index finger, pointing out a buck in the distance. Fran held his breath and looked at his father who stared straight ahead. His father signaled him to raise his rifle. "This one is yours, son. Remember how we practiced. Take one breath, exhale, and squeeze the trigger slowly."

The buck raised its head and seemed to stare right through the nine-year-old boy. Fran looked into the creature's eyes and the rifle seemed to get heavier in his arms the longer he held it. Terrified that he'd lose his nerve and let his father down, he squeezed the trigger.

A loud bang reverberated through the forest, sending dozens of birds fleeing from their perches. The .308 Winchester round slammed into the creature's shoulder, and by the time Fran recovered from the recoil, the deer had gotten back up, and run deeper into the woods in order to escape the hunters.

"Damn it!" His father punched himself in the thigh. "We've got to track it and finish it off. The meat will be ruined, but we can't let it suffer, and we can't let your first kill get away."

They followed the rough, uneven tracks and the trail of blood over equally uneven terrain for what seemed like hours. The autumn sun sank low in the sky by the time they tracked the buck down. Fran begged his father to take the shot and end the hunt with his steady hand and practiced aim, but he insisted that his son take the shot. The more he protested, the shakier his hands got. He pressed the stock of the rifle to his shoulder, tried to aim, and fired again, this time hitting the creature in the neck with a grazing shot that bled profusely, but didn't kill the animal.

"Let's go!" Fran's father had already taken off running. "He won't make it far with a wound like that. We've got to find him before it's pitch black out here."

During their chase, the deer had gotten out of their sight, but they could still hear the general area where it was still limping through the forest. They split up in order to cover more ground and ensure that it didn't outflank them. As the sound of the animal got louder, Fran knew that it had gone in his direction and away from his father. He'd be the one to find it. In the thick brush, the clumsy trudge of the wounded animal ended with a loud thump. Fran rushed towards the sound only able to see the skinny trees silhouetted against the setting sun. He pushed aside the bushes that obscured the dark outline of the buck on its side, breathing weakly. When he pushed past the brush and stood over the creature, he looked down to find a pale naked woman, caked with dirt and jet-black hair veiling her face, hunched over the dying creature. The sight stopped Fran in his tracks. He wanted to call out to his father, but couldn't utter a sound. The impossibly skinny woman looked up from the creature and bared her broken teeth, dripping with blood freshly sucked from the deer's wound. Fran stepped back slowly until he snapped a stick underfoot, which seemed to trigger her movement. The woman stood up and the blood dripped down between her filthy breasts. He turned around to run back the way he'd come but immediately ran face first into a thick, unmovable tree. Fran fell to the ground with blood dripping from a cut in his forehead. His vision clouded with darkness and he felt a warm wetness in his pants. The blackness at the edge of his vision crawled towards the center and his world slipped away into unconsciousness.

Fran's father found him mere moments later. He saw his son out cold on the forest floor with a knife in the his hands. His eyes quickly shot over to the deer which had its throat cut and had been dragged facing downhill. He'd told Fran that if he ever killed a deer to cut the throat and make sure it faced downhill so the blood could drain from the body and prevent the meat from spoiling, but he honestly didn't think that his boy had it in him to actually go through with it. He figured that Fran had done what he had to do and then got lightheaded and fell down. He couldn't decide if he was proud of his son for doing what he'd been taught to do, or ashamed that he'd passed out after having gone through with it. As he thought about it, Fran's father noticed an expanding dark puddle coming from his son's jeans and dripping onto the forest floor.

"Jesus Christ! You pissed yourself." He heard the gruff, but familiar voice scold. "Go to the stream a quarter mile west of here and clean yourself up. I've got to field dress this buck before the meat goes bad. At least you dragged it so it was facing downhill before you cut its throat."

"I didn't," Fran started before realizing that the deer's throat had been cut. He looked down at his right hand to find his partially serrated folding knife caked in blood and placed in his palm. His mind raced with things that he couldn't bring himself to say. He wanted to tell his father that he was a jerk for not even asking if he was okay. He wanted to say that he didn't kill the deer, but more than anything, Fran wanted to tell his father what he'd seen, but he knew that his dad wouldn't believe it. For that matter, Fran wasn't sure if he even believed it. He tried to rationalize it all, reasoning that maybe he'd tripped and hit his head, and dreamed the whole thing when he was knocked out.

They wrapped the buck in a cheap tarp and dragged it to the edge of the forest, where Fran waited for his father to pull up the pickup truck right next to it so they could haul it into the bed of the truck and drive it across the street to Fran's grandmother's house, where they strung it up from the top of the deck so they could skin it, and carve off the various parts of it that his father told him would make the best meals. They cut two steaks from the creature's hind legs. "These will be our dinner tonight." They wrapped the rest in freezer paper and stocked the large freezer chest that had been in Fran's grandmother's basement as long as he could remember.

That night, while Fran's mother, Rosa and grandmother whom he simply called Abuela stayed inside, the two men stood outside over the grill where the venison steaks grilled. Fran's father took them off the grill when they were medium rare. Fran cut into the steak, put a thick chunk of it into his mouth and chewed. The juice dropping down his chin made the image of the woman he'd seen in the forest flash through his mind.

"It tastes weird. Not like when you've brought home venison before. It's not spicy, but...I don't know how to describe it."

"The word you're looking for is, acrid. That's what happens when you don't kill it in one shot." His father explained.

"Why does it do that?" Fran cringed.

"A scientist would tell you that it's lactic acid getting into the muscle tissue, but a hunter would tell you that it's fear you're tasting."

2

"I'm telling you. On the night of the blood moon, a bunch of chicks go out in the woods and dance naked around a big tree in the middle of a clearing," a boy named Jack, a few years older than the twelve-year-old Fran announced. Fran always thought that Jack would grow up to be movie-star handsome and end up with a perfect life. Even as kids, things seemed to always work out for Jack. Fran often felt like his was merely an inhabitant of Jack's world.

"That's bullshit," another boy named Charlie protested.

"It's true. Victor told me before he moved away. Fran, you know these woods pretty good. Right?"

"I guess so." Fran shrugged.

"You ever seen a big clearing with a huge freaking tree in the middle of it?" Jack stood close enough to Fran to emphasize how much taller than Fran he was.

"I think so. I've seen a big tree with a stone fire pit near it," Fran answered.

Charlie stood taller. "Do you think that's what Victor was talking about?"

"It's got to be," Jack exclaimed. "The blood moon is this Thursday. Get your binoculars, your walkie-talkie, and some dark clothes. Tell your grandma we're going camping and we'll have a hell of a show!"

Two nights later, the boys met at the edge of the woods as the sun began to set. Fran walked since it was just across the street from his grandmother's house where he'd spent most of his summer vacations. The other boys rode their bikes.

"I can just show you guys where the tree is, and then I'll go back," Fran squeaked. "I mean...I don't have a sleeping bag or anything."

"Come on Fran. Don't be a wimp." Charlie shoved his shoulder. Charlie was a year older than Jack but they were in the same class since Charlie stayed back a year in second grade. Despite being older, Charlie was a few inches shorter than Jack, and he used an abrasive sense of humor to compensate for his lack of size. When Fran's mother saw glimpses of this, she'd quietly refer to him as Napoleon when talking to Fran about it.

Jack stood between the other two boys, clearly the leader of the group. "Back off, Charlie. Fran's going to stick it out with us. Right, Fran?"

"Right," Fran replied, realizing he had no choice.

The three boys crept through the woods, following Fran's directions. Despite the bright summer sun, the forest floor always seemed to be cloaked in shadow by the thick canopy of trees. The foliage was greener and more alive in the summer, and it barely resembled the dying autumnal abyss that it had been a few years earlier when he'd gone hunting for the first and last time with his father.

"Why do they dance naked in the middle of the woods?" Charlie wondered aloud.

"Don't you know anything?" Jack scoffed. "They're witches or whatever. They go out and worship the trees instead of going to church or something like that."

"Weird." Charlie marveled.

"I hear lots of them are lesbians. Maybe we'll see some action." Jack teased. "You heard that before. Right, Fran?"

"Yeah. Totally." Fran agreed even though he'd never heard anything like that before. He went along with it because he'd never dare disagree with a kid like Jack. It wasn't that Jack was intimidating. It was simply that everyone admired him to the point where the simple act of disagreeing with him seemed wrong.

The three boys stopped when they stumbled into a clearing with a tree at least five times bigger than any other tree in the forest and a circle of stones with charred logs resting in the center of the circle.

"That tree's freaking huge!" Charlie exclaimed.

"I told you!" Jack asserted. "Now let's find spots for each of us to hide out."

"What do you mean?" Fran's voice shuddered.

Jack put a hand on each of the other boy's shoulders. "Well, we can't all squat behind the same tree...Besides, I don't want to be anywhere near Charlie if he gets a chub tonight."

"Shut up!" Charlie punched Jack on the shoulder.

Jack led the boys through the area surrounding the clearing and found spots for each of them to hide. Charlie climbed up a tree and sat between two branches that cradled him and kept him out of sight. Jack ducked in the space between two large rocks that had wedged together to make a tiny cave that he could cloister himself inside. Fran crawled on his stomach underneath some brush that obscured his view. He figured that if he couldn't see the clearing, then nobody in the clearing could see him. That rationalization gave him the only semblance of comfort that he figured he'd have that night. He remembered the woman that he'd seen, hunched over the deer he'd shot years earlier and prayed that she wasn't one of the women that apparently visited the forest at night.

The sun sank behind the horizon, and scenarios of everything that could go wrong ran through Fran's mind. What if they saw him and hurt him? What if they took him to the police and everyone knew he was peeping like a pervert? What if he got scared and ran and the boys called him a chicken? What if they used his blood to do some sort of ritual? He grabbed handfuls of leaves and covered himself as best he could.

Fran promised himself that he wouldn't run away. He couldn't show his face to the other kids in the neighborhood if Jack and Charlie told anyone that he ran and they stuck it out. He didn't care about seeing some naked girls in the dark. He just wanted to make it through the night without anyone accusing him of being either a coward or a creep.

With the last moments of dying light, Fran looked towards the places he saw Jack and Charlie hide and made sure that he couldn't see them. He rationalized that if he couldn't see them, then they couldn't see him. When he knew that nobody could see him, he buried his face in the leaves, and closed his eyes, hoping the night would end quickly.

He woke up when an orange glow rose up in the pitch-black forest, making shadows dance along with the women making them. His left arm tingled and he figured that he'd fallen asleep on it and it had gone numb. The fire in the darkness made silhouettes of them that reminded him of the shadow puppetry that his second-grade teacher did four years earlier. Female voices chanted in a language that he couldn't recognize.

Suddenly the fire flashed like a flare before going out instantly, not like when he'd thrown buckets of water on campfires previous summers. This looked more like a lightbulb going out. After a few seconds of perfect silence and darkness that felt like an hour, new voices pierced the blank slate of the night. Their accent sounded like they were from England or Ireland and their language was full of the thous and thys of the bible. Their angry shouting was punctuated by the sound of axes chopping wood, and the creak of logs being bundled together. The fire shot straight up the stem of a tree that had been propped up by other branches and steadied with ropes. He watched as the massive log burned, but the shadow told a different story. The shadow cast by the burning log showed four women, one on each side of the log writhing as they burned, lashed to the sturdy branch. Fran wanted to look to see where Jack and the others were, but he didn't dare move.

"Without us thou art doomed! The spirits of the wild shall feast upon thee." an agonized female voice wailed.

"It is thou that art doomed, thou fallen wench!" a man's voice shouted.

The dull ache in Fran's left arm intensified and he rolled up his black hoodie's sleeve and examined his left forearm. A bumpy half circle bruise formed on his forearm, and he recognized it as a bite mark of his own making. He'd heard of people scratching themselves in their sleep, but never biting themselves. He rubbed his sore forearm and tucked it under his body as he watched from beneath the brush, frozen with fear. But again, the fire, the sound, all of it, went out in an instant. Convinced that each twig snapping or leaf crunching was one of them searching for him. He buried his face in the leaves and prayed that nobody could see him.

As Fran lay there, the pale grey light of the morning faded into view he lifted his head and scanned the area. There were no burnt pillars, no crisped bodies, nothing but a symbol burned into the gigantic tree in the form of a large letter "X" with a diamond shape cradled in the space above the intersection of the two lines. He stood up and warily inched forward towards the tree, extending his hand as if touching the symbol would confirm whether it was real.

When he touched the bottom of the "X" symbol, the black burn mark slithered up his right arm, towards his face. Fran fell onto his back and closed his eyes tightly as he frantically swiped at his arm. He opened his eyes and looked down at his arms, and then back at the tree. Not only was there nothing on his arms other than the bruise left by his own bite mark on his left arm, but there was also no evidence that the symbol had ever been burned into the bark of the tree. Fran ran towards the edge of the forest, where Jack and Charlie left their bikes.

When he got to the edge of the road, where the forest ended and civilization took over, Jack and Charlie's bikes were gone from the trees that they'd locked them to the night before. When Fran saw that, he realized that he hadn't even attempted to see if they were still around. He hoped they weren't. That way, nobody would have witnessed him freak out on the ground when he thought there was something on his arm.

Before heading home, he found them at the back of the local grocery store trying to jump their skateboards down the short set of stairs that led up to the loading docks. It was their usual Friday morning hangout during the summers.

Jack landed with bent knees after jumping his skateboard off the loading dock and he made eye contact with Fran. "Jesus, Fran. You look like hell."

Fran grumbled. "How come you guys weren't there this morning?"

"Wait...You mean to tell me you actually stayed out there all night?" Charlie looked Fran up and down before breaking into merciless peals of laughter.

"You said you were going to stay out there. You had me tell my grandma that I was staying at your house tonight," Fran stammered.

Jack cut in, equally cruel but with a politeness to it that made him automatically seem right in whatever he said. "Look. We ditched you at midnight when we figured nobody was going to show up and that Victor was a liar, but we were just messing with you. We thought you'd follow us out a few minutes later. When you didn't, we had to leave. There's no way we could have found that clearing again without you."

Fran couldn't say anything. Jack phrased his interpretation of what happened in such a way that Fran felt stupid for disagreeing with him. Charlie's merciless laughter just made Fran want the joke to be over as quickly as possible, and he knew that saying anything to him would be seen as whining and would give Charlie more material for jokes at his expense. He didn't dare tell them about the fire and the shadows or about the screaming and the burning. He could just see Charlie berating him, saying that he had a bad dream when he was asleep face down in the dirt. That would be worse than anything. Fran knew he had to walk away.

"I need a shower." Fran turned and walked down the sidewalk towards his grandmother's house, without giving the boys an opportunity to say anything else.

By the time Fran had cleaned himself up and changed his clothes, his mom came to pick him up from his grandma's house for the weekend. During the school year, he spent the week at home, and the weekends at his grandma's house. When it was summer vacation, it was the opposite. Fran's parents told him that it was because his grandma's neighborhood was more fun in the summer because of the forest, the swimming hole, and the neighborhood kids, but after a few years of this routine, Fran started to think that his parents just liked having more time to themselves over the summer. He didn't mind though, because he lived on a long straight road with no sidewalks. People drove way too fast on the road so it wasn't the best place to ride a bicycle. This neighborhood not only had sidewalks and neighborhood kids, but it also had a handful of places that he could get to without the help of an adult. With the help of his bicycle and the neighborhood kids, he could get to the forest, the swimming hole, the convenience store, and the old drive-in movie theater.

They drove in silence for the first ten minutes out of the forty-minute drive back to their house, but then he had to ask. "Mom? Is it true what they say about the woods near grandma's house?"

"What do they say?" his mother asked. She brushed her curly hair out of her face, which looked beautiful but tired.

"That there's witches in the woods. I know it sounds crazy, but when we were going hiking, the guys said that they come out during the full moon."

"And let me guess," his mother interrupted. "Last night was a full moon. Right?"

"...Yeah."

"Sounds like they pulled a prank on you, Frannie."

Fran hated when she called him Frannie, and it embarrassed him that she was probably right. He pivoted his questioning to make himself sound less scared than he was. "I know, Mom. I just mean, do you think their prank was based on anything real?"

His mother considered his question and how best to answer it. "Back in settler times some of the Pilgrims found out that girls in this town were practicing witchcraft, and they burned them at the stake. Jack and Charlie's families have lived in this town for a very long time, so they probably heard the old ghost story when they were little, and they used it to scare you."

"So, this town was like Salem? Why isn't it famous then?"

"Salem was a big town back in those times, and the witch trials made it famous. There weren't any trials with this group. A big angry mob got together and killed those poor girls for believing something different. That's why you don't hear about it. Because it was a shameful thing that they did. It's something that the town wants the world to forget."

They drove in silence, until Fran's mom pulled off the highway and made her way towards their neighborhood. "So, what did they do to try to scare you?"

Fran described a version of the previous night that was mostly true. He left out the part about them trying to peep on the women in the woods, and told her that they just wanted to go camping. He described the lights, the shadows, and the sounds. Fran's mother regarded the story with amusement, almost as if she approved of the prank.

"You'll have to get them back. I'm going to buy you something." Fran's mom stopped at a side of the road stand that was selling fireworks for the fourth of July and she bought him a dozen tiny firecrackers that would make a loud bang when the strings on either side of them were pulled tightly enough to break the firecracker. She showed him how to tape them to doors so that they would go off when someone opened the door. Fran figured he wouldn't end up using them to get back at Charlie and Jack, but he liked playing as if he would with his mother.

He liked to pretend he was the hero, dispensing justice with a strong will and whatever superpowers he imagined. During the days it made him feel assertive and strong. It was only in the quiet of the night that a small voice in his head would tell him that it was just a fantasy.

3

Brad Catcher felt stupid begging his older brother for anything, especially when his friends, Fran and Charlie were around. It took an hour and a pep talk from his girlfriend to build up the willpower to knock on Jack's bedroom door, where he was playing video games with his friends and to ask to borrow Jack's new car. In the end, it wasn't half as big a deal to Jack as it was to Brad. Then again, Brad's older brother never seemed to let anything get to him.

"Bring it back in one piece." Jack Catcher tossed his younger brother Brad the keys to his 1999 Ford Focus, which he'd worked the entire summer to save up to buy.

"Thanks so much, Jack. This really means a lot." Brad wrapped an arm around his older brother, still clutching the keys in his hand. He didn't particularly like driving. If it were up to him, he'd just walk around town like he'd been doing ever since he got together with his girlfriend, Audrey.

When they got together back in eighth grade simply because he was the only boy in class with a mohawk and she was the only girl in class with hair dyed pink. They spent their afternoons listening to Rancid and NOFX in Brad's basement which had been refurbished into a second living room in his parents' house.

Their relationship grew over the three years that they spent nearly every day together. It started out as making out and listening to music, and shifted into smoking weed, having sex, and talking about the day when they wouldn't have to deal with high school any longer. They talked about moving out to San Francisco and getting a little apartment and hanging out with the hippies, punks, and burnouts and loving every minute of it.

They'd done everything together since the day they met and they were on their way to another experience together, their first concert in Boston. Brad had taken his driving test four times before he could pass and got his driver's license just in time to drive them to Boston to see Against Me playing at the House of Blues.

Brad had been devastated when he didn't pass his driving test the first time, not because he cared about driving, but because he felt like he'd let Audrey down. In that moment, he felt utterly broken, but at the same time it made him realize for the first time that he cared more about Audrey than he cared about himself. He'd learned the lesson through pain, but he felt lucky to care about someone so much. After another three tries, he finally parallel parked correctly and got his license. When he got home, Audrey was there waiting for him. They curled up on the worn old couch in the basement and stared at her phone looking through the list of bands they liked that would be coming through the area. Against Me was on tour promoting their new album, *White Crosses* and would be playing at the House of Blues in Boston, a mere hour drive from Hopeville. They made a pact to go together, just the two of them, and to spend the weekend together.

When they found a place to park their car, Audrey led Brad around Boston without looking up from the navigation app on her phone. They found the venue just as the sun began to set behind the brick building. They disappeared into the sea of leather jackets and Doc Martens and ended up hanging out with a group of street punks in a blue spray-painted van. When Brad sat down with Audrey in his lap and looked around the inside, he was fairly certain that they lived in the van. They passed around cans of PBR, a cheap bottle of whiskey, and a joint.

"This is way stronger than the stuff we get back home." Audrey coughed.

A spikey haired man took the joint from her, took a long toke of it and asked, "Where are you two from?"

"Hopeville, Massachusetts." Audrey replied with a tone of voice bordering on disgust.

"Oh. You're country kids," a girl with a snakebite piercing teased.

Brad wanted to assert that Hopeville wasn't the country, but he didn't think that insisting that they were from the suburbs would sound any better, so he simply asked where they were from.

"Well Scott and I are from New London, Connecticut," the girl with the snakebite piercing said, gesturing to one of the guys in the van. "The rest of these fuckers are from Worcester, Massachusetts. We had a little folk-punk duo, but when the El N Gee closed and a big chunk of the punk scene died with it, we moved up to Massachusetts and found Neil to play bass, and Adam to play drums."

Audrey was suddenly fascinated that they were in a van that a folk-punk band probably toured in. "What do you two play?"

Scott slapped a guitar case that he rested his back against. "I play guitar, and Janie plays mandolin and sings."

"That's so cool!" Audrey exclaimed as she finished her second beer.

When Brad took another pull from the bottle of whiskey, he saw Neil climb into the front seat of the van and open up a package of cold medicine. "You feeling alright?" he asked.

"Oh, we're fine. These red devils are just to take the show to the next level," Neil said, as if those few words would make Audrey and Brad understand.

"Red devils?" Audrey asked, intuitively knowing that Brad would feel too self-conscious to admit that he didn't know what that meant.

Janie shuffled over next to Audrey and explained that taking too many of a certain type of cold pill could get you high. "Adam and Neil like it, but I can't enjoy a show when it looks like the stage is moving back and forth like waves."

"Yeah." Audrey shrugged. "We might try that back home, but not tonight. I've never seen Against Me before, and I want to really remember every moment of it."

They finished smoking, and the beers were empty shortly thereafter and they filed into the venue and lost the others in the crowd. Brad figured that they'd never see the four from the van again, and smirked to himself thinking about all the characters that would come and go during their life together in San Francisco.

The opening act played a brand of punk rock that was more political, but less catchy than Against Me, and Brad decided that he liked them a lot, but understood why they'd never be as popular as the band he'd come to see. They stuck to the back of the crowd where they had a better view until Audrey took Brad by the hand and pulled him into the women's bathroom, and then into the handicapped stall. They had brief but passionate sex, keeping most of their clothes on and leaning over the railing of the handicapped toilet. The whooping they heard from outside the stall was mostly good natured, and Brad was glad that she dragged him into the women's room instead of the men's. When they went to return to the crowd, Brad had the idea to leave the bathroom one at a time, but Audrey quickly reminded him that nobody there knew them, and it was a punk show, so they probably wouldn't care. They returned to the crowd just as Against Me began their set.

Audrey and Brad bounced, danced, and sang along to the two-hour set of sanctioned chaos. Without trying to, they got shuffled from the back of the crowd to the front row on the right side of the stage, where the lead guitarist, James Bowman who wore his typical uniform of black jeans and a plain black T-shirt and played fast, aggressive riffs. Neither of them could believe how close they ended up, and Audrey took several blurry pictures of James Bowman and the singer Laura Jane Grace, with her sleeve tattoos and long reddish hair. She wanted to use the pictures on her phone to help her remember the night for the rest of her life. During the lull between the band's set and the encore, Brad bought Audrey a black T-shirt with the band's logo on it and an enamel pin in the shape of a black feather for himself. Audrey put the shirt on over her tank top and Brad attached the pin to the collar of his jean jacket.

After the show ended, they climbed back into the Ford and drove east out of Boston, towards Cape Cod. They decided to spend the remainder of the weekend in Provincetown since, from what they understood, it was the San Francisco of the east coast. They spent their days walking around looking at art they couldn't afford, eating seafood, and walking up and down the beach, each of them with an earbud in one ear, playing their favorite music. They found groups of other people their age huddled around bonfires dotting the beach. Occasionally they'd integrate themselves into the groups of teenagers around the bonfires, especially if they had weed, but mostly they kept to themselves, as if the beach belonged to them and the bonfires were merely monuments meant to memorialize their love.

They tried to spend the night curled up under a blanket on the beach, but when the ocean air got too cold, they ended up in the backseat of the car, making love and falling asleep curled up together. When Brad woke up to the scent of Audrey's hair, he knew that nothing could go wrong as long as they were together.

As if he predicted it, Brad was right. The moment he got home from dropping Audrey off, his older brother confronted him about a dent that he hadn't even noticed during the weekend away.

"That's just fucking great, Brad!" Jack scolded. "Now I have to take the blame for you, because if Mom and Dad find out that I loaned you the car to run off for the weekend, it'll be even worse for me."

"I'm sorry, Jack." Brad sighed, trying to hang onto the joy of the weekend.

"Not as sorry as I'm going to be," Jack grunted. "I try to do you a favor, and this is what happens."

"I know it was a favor, and I'll make it up to you. I'll do your homework for however long you're grounded," Brad offered.

"That would be a decent offer if you weren't a C student." Jack bit his lip. "Just don't fuck up like this again."

Over the next several weeks, Brad continued spending as much time as possible with Audrey, but he did so outside of the house. His guilt over Jack having to take the blame for the dent in the Ford's fender felt even worse when Audrey came to the house. Knowing that Jack was grounded while he was able to have her over made it seem even more wrong, and Jack didn't allow Brad any way to make it up to him. They'd exhausted many of the usual places they could hang out without having to spend money or drive. The police told them to steer clear of the local parks after they found that someone drew a dick on the playscape the same night that they were caught on a park bench after dark. The local comic book store demanded that they buy something or leave. Audrey romantically fantasized about finding a spot in the woods where nobody would bother them, where they could set up a little hammock and lay out in the sunshine, and make love all summer. As was always the case when Audrey had a romantic idea, Brad wanted to make it a reality.

He thought for a few moments as they walked, and he froze when the idea struck him. "I know about a big patch of woods where nobody lives. We could find a nice little clearing there and set up your hammock."

"Our hammock." Audrey hugged his arm tightly.

"It's across the street from one of Jack's friend's houses. Let me show you." He led Audrey down a few side streets until they reached the edge of the forest. They hiked a mile into the woods, Audrey leaving a trail of bright pink beads from a bracelet she'd broken every so often to mark their path like *Hansel and Gretel*.

"This is it. This is our spot!" Audrey exclaimed when she found a relatively flat patch of grass with two trees, about ten feet away from each other, perfect for her hammock.

"Do you have a pocket knife?" Brad asked.

"Why would I have a pocket knife? Why do you need one?"

Brad blushed. "I wanted to do that thing couples do, where we carve our initials into a tree."

"You're so cute."

Brad ran his hand through his shaggy hair. "I'll bring a pocket knife next time."

She turned and looked Brad up and down before taking off her top and leading him by the hand to one of the trees. She hung her bra from one of the branches. "I'd plant a flag, but this is the best I've got."

Brad and Audrey spent the rest of the afternoon in the woods, like they were Adam and Eve, the only two people in the world. But as the sun sank closer to the horizon, they knew they'd have to return to the world while they could still see the pink beads in the dirt.

They spent the next week making their own little paradise in the forest. They strung up the wide rope hammock between two trees, carved their names into each of the trees, and cleared all of the rocks and twigs from the small clearing of flat earth so they could walk barefoot comfortably. They sometimes packed picnics, simply so they wouldn't have to cut their time in the forest short to get dinner. Afternoons spent in their personal Garden of Eden were some of the happiest that Brad had ever experienced.

After making love in the hammock, they held one another and stared at the sheltered blue sky, and said nothing. Audrey slowly raised her head when she heard a twig snap in the distance. She saw a buck, about five feet tall at the shoulder with antlers reach towards the heavens, and she gently stroked Brad's hand to get his attention. He looked up and together they watched it gracefully wander through their paradise, sniffing at their pile of clothing and looking at them, its senses alert and waiting for any sign of a threat.

The buck stood, regarding them just long enough for Brad to think about the peace that would have to exist in a person's heart for them to exist harmoniously with animals in a forest, before it turned and trotted away from their paradise.

"The antler man approves," Audrey declared. "The forest wants us here."

"What do you mean?" Brad asked, still looking in the direction that the buck had gone.

"The wendigo, the spirit of the forest. Some Native American tribes around here believed in it. They say it looked like a man with antlers, representing the merging of humanity and the natural world. That's why I called it the antler man." After getting her DNA tested, Audrey found out that she was part Native American and she'd begun trying to learn as much as she could about the local tribes. Her research hadn't gone much deeper than a few Google searches and websites with varying degrees of credibility, but she figured that she had to start somewhere.

"Is it supposed to be a good spirit or a bad spirit?" Brad scanned his eyes back and forth looking for the animal.

"Some believed that it was a guardian of the forest, and that you have nothing to fear from it, so long as you respect its forest. Other tribes saw it as a man-eating forest spirit, representing greed, murder, and cannibalism," she explained.

"Cheery thought." Brad tried to chuckle.

"Personally, I think it mirrors a person's intentions. If you're malicious, it'll come in the form of a monster. If you live peacefully, then it might take the form of...our friend there." Audrey gestured in the direction the buck had run.

Back at his house, Brad told his brother about their experience in the forest and about the legend that Audrey shared with him. He did all this while he cleaned Jack's room. Cleaning his brother's room was just one of the handful of gestures and favors Brad had been doing for Jack ever since Jack got grounded when he took the blame for Brad denting the car.

"Dude. I like Audrey, but I can't figure her out," Jack mused. "She looks like a punk, but the way she talks...sounds like a total hippie."

Brad smirked at his brother's assessment of his girlfriend. "I guess when you think about it, the only difference between a punk and a hippie is that the punk is angrier."

"That and the music is faster." Jack flashed a quick smile, which he hid as quickly as he could. He'd been trying to stay mad at his brother, but couldn't help but feel happy for his misfit brother being so in love. "Maybe that can be your band's name if you ever put one together. The Antler Men."

"I'll never get a band together." Brad strained to reach a piece of crumpled paper that had been kicked deep under Jack's bed. "First, I'd have to stop sucking at guitar, and then I'd need to find a drummer and a bass player that will go along with all the weird punk-hippie ideas in my head."

"Just keep dicking around on that acoustic in your room and you'll be able to complete the trifecta. Sex, drugs, *and* rock and roll." Jack tousled his brother's shaggy hair.

Back at their paradise, Audrey opened a package of the cold medicine that the kids in the van nicknamed Red Devils and put a handful of them in Brad's hand. He looked down at the small red pills and realized that this would be the first drug he'd done that could kill him. He knew he couldn't overdose on weed, and he never had enough money to buy enough alcohol to really get sick. These pills were supposed to make you feel better, and only became recreational when you took too many. It reminded him of the title of a song that Jack liked, "The Difference Between Medicine and Poison is the Dose" by the band, Circa Survive.

He asked, "How do we know if we take too many?"

"Taking too many is kind of the point." Audrey smirked. "But I looked it up. This much should give us a trip, but won't land us in the emergency room."

"How do we make it stop if we don't like it?" Brad stared at the pills, which had begun to feel heavy in his hand.

Audrey gestured to the two-gallon jugs of water she'd brought with her. "Just drink a lot of water and your system will flush it out sooner. Don't be so paranoid."

He took the handful of pills with two big gulps of the water and watched Audrey do the same. At first, nothing happened and they lay in the hammock looking at the sky. Clouds encircled the sun and muted the light of the forest, giving the forest a gray tone that almost made it look like a black and white photo. Brad wondered aloud how much of what he was seeing was actually there and how much was in his head.

Audrey got out of the hammock and looked around, and danced in a spinning motion as she hummed a playful tune that Brad didn't recognize, but knew he'd never forget. She approached a tree and felt the bark. "Is that really there?"

"The tree?" Brad asked.

"The boards nailed into the tree," she said. "Like when people nail boards to a tree to make a ladder to a treehouse."

Brad reached out and felt nothing but the rough bark of the tree. "I don't feel anything. No boards. No treehouse."

"I want a treehouse," Audrey whined.

Brad held her close. "Maybe we'll live in a log cabin someday. That's kind of like a treehouse."

"A log cabin in San Francisco? I'm not high enough to think that there's cabins in that city." She laughed.

They wandered the forest, never losing sight of their hammock. They experimented with different ideas and with each other, wondering if sex felt different with that kind of high. Brad stood over Audrey as she lay on her back across the width of the hammock. Brad felt the first few raindrops on his bare skin, but Audrey didn't notice it at first. He nibbled at her neck more aggressively than he'd done before, and the rational part of his mind, hidden behind the lust that had taken over wondered if the urge came from the lack of inhibition that the pills had given him, or had the blurred line between sex and violence always there?

Audrey leaned her head back over the edge of the hammock with her eyes closed. She let out a cry of animalistic pleasure and when she opened her eyes her pleasure turned into terror. The tall human shape with black leathery skin clinging to its emaciated body stood over her with its antlers mingling with the low branches of the trees. She screamed and rolled away from Brad, flipping out of the hammock and falling into the dirt. Audrey scrambled across the ground to her clothes and pulled on her underwear and her top.

Brad didn't see the antler man, or anything besides Audrey's body and the swirling lattice of the hammock that he took for a hallucination. What he knew for sure was that his girlfriend had seen something that terrified her, and that in all likelihood, whatever she saw wasn't really there. He rushed to her, pulling on his boxer shorts and his t-shirt, but not feeling any less naked. Brad tried to take Audrey in his arms, struggling to push his own hallucinations out of his mind so he could help Audrey deal with her own.

"Brad. We have to get the fuck out of here!" Audrey pleaded. "The antler man is here and he's going to kill us."

The sky opened up and started pouring rain onto them, turning the dirt into mud and the rocks into slippery traps that could cause a catastrophic crash with one misplaced step. Brad looked at Audrey's face and then followed her gaze deeper into the forest and he saw the antler man too. He didn't have time to consider what it meant that they both saw it because the creature dropped onto all fours and scrambled up a tree far too narrow to support its weight like a bug climbing the leg of a chair.

Audrey ran through the rain and the mud with Brad following behind. Neither of them dared look back, but they heard the treetops sway and rustle as if the creature followed them, jumping from branch to branch, preparing to pounce when it got close enough. Brad could barely see

Audrey in front of him and he wondered when it got so
dark. He wondered if more time had passed while they
were high than he thought. He thought about the
possibility that he might still be hallucinating and that the
creature that hunted them may not actually exist. With that
thought, Brad decided that he would keep that in mind and
not do anything that relied on the wendigo being real. He
rationalized that running out of the woods and sobering up
somewhere else would be fine, and going to the police
station screaming about a monster in the woods would not.

They neared the street and despite sheets of rain
coming down hard, Brad could see headlights coming
down the street fast.

"Audrey! Stop!" He shouted as he ran into the street
after her.

Brad wrapped his arms around Audrey for the last
time, trying to pull her out of the path of the speeding car,
but it was too late. The bumper of the sedan snapped both
of Brad's legs halfway up the shin bone causing him to fall
forward onto the hood of the car and smash his brow into
the windshield that broke with the impact. Audrey's thigh
took the brunt of the car's impact, breaking her leg midway
up causing the bone to stab through the flesh and stick out
from the wound that spurted gouts of blood from her

severed femoral artery. She would have bled to death in mere minutes, but her body was thrown away from the crash, back towards the woods, where her head hit the side of a tree, causing her neck to break with a sickening cracking sound that served as the last sound Brad would hear before passing out. He lay on the hood of the car, his vision fading, and saw the antler man standing at the edge of the treeline standing over Audrey's lifeless body, but not making any movements towards her.

Brad woke up with his senses gradually returning to him. First, he noticed harsh fluorescent lighting. Then he heard the beeping of his slowly increasing heart rate on a monitor, and finally he registered the familiar smell of his mother, her perfume mixed with the campfire smell from the fireplace in their home. His vision came into focus and he saw his parents and brother standing over him. When he tried to speak, he felt something in his throat and began gagging and retching. A nurse held a plastic pan in front of his mouth and he vomited a thick black substance that looked like tar into it. His eyes widened in horror as memories of what happened to him and Audrey flooded back and he tried to figure out what the grainy oil coming out of his mouth could be. At first, he thought that it was some sort of concentrated evil that the forest demon put into him, but then he remembered getting out of the woods. Then he remembered the headlights coming at him and Audrey.

"What?" Brad started to form a longer question, but his throat felt like he'd swallowed a fistful of sand.

The nurse stood over him, having seen this situation many times before in the emergency room. "It's charcoal. You were on the verge of an overdose when we picked you up. The girl had a ton in her system too."

"Aud--" He tried to say her name, but couldn't get it out.

"Audrey died in the car crash, honey." Brad's mother said. "Did you and Audrey have some kind of suicide pact?"

There followed a silence that only lasted a few seconds, but felt like a thousand years to Brad. His world, past present and future, shattered. He'd never live in San Francisco. He'd never marry Audrey and start a quirky but functional family. He'd never be able to close his eyes without seeing her standing in the headlights of that car. Brad had just found out that he'd survived getting hit by a car, but immediately wished that he hadn't. He'd lost the one person who ever really understood him. Even his own mother assumed that he had some sort of suicide pact with Audrey. He wanted to tell her the truth, but even if he could form the words, he knew that saying that they were simply trying to get high wouldn't sound any better. Nobody would understand that summer in the forest except Audrey, partly because she'd been there, but mostly because she knew him, heart and soul, in a way that nobody else ever could. Instead, he said nothing and when he tried to move, a sharp pain set his legs on fire.

"Easy, buddy." Jack said with a calming tone. "Don't try to move. You busted up your legs pretty bad."

Brad's eyes widened and he looked at his father, looking strong but on the edge of falling apart at the same time. His dad always looked just like Jack, except with a potbelly and a single tattoo on his forearm, memorializing his time in the military. Brad knew that he wouldn't sugarcoat what had happened to him.

His father sighed. "They're both broken. You'll walk again, but not for a while. And until you're okay again, we'll be there for you."

Brad nodded. He didn't have the heart, or the ability to tell his father that he'd never be okay again, but he accepted his family's support. They visited him as often as they were allowed to. His father took time off and delegated many of his responsibilities to his friend Brody who had started working for Brad's grandfather when he ran Catcher Construction and Tree Removal, usually shortened to simply Catcher Construction and had stuck around that entire time, his only time away from the company had been when he was drafted to fight in Vietnam. Jack stopped at the hospital on his way home from school to see how his brother's physical therapy had been going.

When his family visited, Brad told them what they wanted to hear, but never the story of what had happened, and never the full extent of his thoughts. He promised himself never to tell them about the paradise that he and Audrey created, he'd never say anything about the antler man, and that the only time he could stop thinking about that night was when he was full of painkillers. He remained faithful to that promise until after ten years of addiction that started out as a dependency on prescription painkillers and eventually became full blown heroin addiction, when he made it to the fifth step of recovery when he had to tell another person about his wrongdoings, which had multiplied and worsened over the years. That was when he told his brother Jack about that summer, about that night, and about the antler man.

4

"Rivera! You're late and Flynn's computer keeps crashing. Get back to your cubicle."

"Sorry, Mr. Archer. My grandmother's really sick and it took longer to get her through the morning routine than I hoped," Fran explained.

"Don't let it happen again. Get one of the dozens of cousins you probably have to handle it," Mr. Archer scolded.

"It won't happen again." Fran bowed his head and meekly shuffled to his desk. He opened up the program that allowed him to access Mr. Flynn's computer remotely, since this was hardly his first time falling for a phishing scam that gave the company computer a virus. Fran also opened up a second tab where he added his boss's latest racist comment to a growing list of mistreatments and abuses he'd suffered in the three years he'd worked at the company. He always told himself that if the company ever tried to get rid of him, he'd use the documentation of racism within the company as leverage to help himself. Fran often fantasized about printing out the document and slamming it down on Mr. Archer's desk, but deep down he knew that it was just that. A fantasy.

He skimmed through the document, which he had titled, "My Escape Plan" and put the latest comment underneath the previous Friday's comment in which Mr. Archer threatened to pull up his pickup truck at Home Depot to find a replacement for him.

Fran split his time between solving problems, preventing problems, and checking the video monitoring system he'd installed at his grandmother's house so he could check in on her. He knew that he couldn't do anything except make a phone call for a small problem or call 911 for a big one.

He went out to the deli down the street to buy his lunch, even though he packed himself one. He just needed to get out of the building for a break. Another reason he went to the same deli every time he either forgot to pack a lunch or needed to get away was that he had a crush on the girl who worked the lunch rush there. She had blonde hair in a pixie cut and the most perfect smile he'd ever seen. He'd been buying turkey sandwiches from her for a year and each session of small talk as she made the sandwich became a little boost that got him through the second half of the day. He'd learned a lot about her over the months he'd been going there, but all she knew was that he liked turkey sandwiches with extra mayo and that he worked down the street. Today he couldn't let the small talk distract him from his morning. It wasn't just that his boss was a racist asshole. It was that Mr. Archer completely disregarded his grandmother's failing health by not even taking it into consideration when he talked to him. It made him feel like a statistic, a replaceable office drone.

On his walk back to work, Fran checked the live video of his grandmother's living room. She wasn't there. Back when he first put the system in place, it would have worried him, but after three months of failing health and watching the video, he knew that she was likely just in the bathroom and would return to her rocking chair and her game shows soon. He didn't worry until he got back to his desk and checked the video again. Either she'd been in the bathroom for half an hour, or something was wrong.

He called her house phone twice before opening the security system's app on the phone and calling out to her through the intercom system. "Grandma? Are you there?"

Silence.

He tried again, with no reply. Fran took in every detail that the two camera angles would show him. She wasn't on the couch, in her rocking chair, or in bed. There was no reason she'd be in the kitchen so long, and it wasn't likely she'd spend an hour in the bathroom.

Fran thought back on all the weekends he'd spent at her house, and came up with one more idea. He called out to her in her first language. "¡Abuela! ¿Estás bien? ¿Estás a salvo?"

He repeated the phrase in a hushed whisper, slowly building up into a shout until Mr. Archer stood over him in his cubicle.

"What are you doing now? You trying to talk your mother through setting up the DVD player? Who am I kidding? I doubt they even have DVD players in Mexico."

Fran stood up and found himself nose to nose with Mr. Archer before he had a chance to talk himself out of it. "First of all, I'm not even Mexican. Second, I need to send my grandmother an ambulance. Third of all, if you're smart, you'll cut the racist bullshit out before it comes back to haunt you." He stormed off and dialed 911 on his phone as he rushed to his car.

He made what was normally a twenty-minute drive from work to his grandmother's house in fifteen minutes, rushing through yellow lights and ignoring speed limit signs. Despite all this, the paramedics beat him to the house by mere moments. They wouldn't let him into the bedroom where they found her as one of them performed CPR. When they realized that the old woman was beyond saving, one of the paramedics walked Fran to the front door of the house and explained that she'd likely had a stroke standing over the bed. Being told that she died instantly and didn't suffer didn't give him any relief.

When he returned to work the next day, Fran didn't intend to stay for the day. He just planned to go to the Human Resources department to fill out the necessary paperwork to take a short leave of absence to see to his grandmother's funeral arrangements. However, he couldn't make it to the HR department to find the paperwork; Mr. Archer and a security guard waited for him at his desk. The security guard's hand rested on the pepper spray holstered in his belt, as if he wished Fran would do something that would give him an excuse to use it.

The security guard handed Fran a document on company stock saying that his threatening comments towards Mr. Archer were inappropriate and his position had been terminated.

Fran went along with the security guard and asked if he could get something off the computer before he left. When he went to approach the computer, the security guard stood between Fran and the computer.

"You were also using a work computer for personal business, so the computer is being brought to an independent consultant to make sure that nothing like this happens again."

"This is crazy!" Fran shouted, realizing that his only chance to save his career lay in the evidence on the computer. "I need five minutes on the computer. You can watch me over my shoulder the whole time."

The security guard put his right hand on Fran's shoulder, halting him. His other hand gripped the pepper spray holstered on his belt. "You aren't permitted near any company equipment. You're leaving now, one way or another."

When Fran shrugged his shoulders in defeat and began to follow the guard out the building, he shot one last defeated glance at Mr. Archer and saw him grin. That was when Fran realized what had happened. He'd rushed out of the building so quickly that he didn't remember to close the window on his computer documenting his boss's interactions with him. Mr. Archer must have seen it and found a way to get rid of him as quickly as possible. If the independent consultant he planned to give the computer to existed at all, they'd be tasked with erasing any trace of Fran's evidence. He knew that it was more likely that Mr. Archer would just have the computer destroyed along with any hope Fran had of saving himself.

Fran never drank much but told himself that after the last two days, he needed it. He drove to his studio apartment and then trudged to a bar down the street called Knuckleheads that had an unmistakably rock and roll sensibility that made him feel like a pussy. He ran the events of the morning through his mind and thought of all the ways he should have stood up for himself. Anything would have been better than what he'd done. A bartender with arms full of tattoos and mutton chops asked what he wanted to drink.

"Something cheap and strong," Fran said without making eye contact. "My grandma died yesterday, and I got fired this morning."

The bartender poured a shot of bourbon for Fran, and another for himself. "This one's on the house, dude."

"Thanks."

The tattooed man raised his shot glass. "I hope you told them to go fuck themselves."

"I wish," Fran replied as they both downed the liquor.

The bartender, Johan, saw that Fran needed to think about something to distract him from the one-two-punch he'd suffered over the last twenty-four hours, so he talked about the band that would be playing the following weekend, and his latest run-throughs of video games that they'd both played when they were kids. Fran appreciated the conversation, and actually managed a smile when a second bartender came in and turned on the song Kick Start My Heart, which prompted Johan to crack open a hard-iced tea and chug it down in mere seconds. It seemed that they had some sort of ongoing drinking game going in which one bartender came in to relieve the other one, and if they played the song without them noticing, they'd have to clock out for the night and down the drink before the first verse ended. The deep unspoken camaraderie between the two men both encouraged Fran that not everyone was bad, and made him wish he had something like that in his life.

Two hours and five drinks later, Fran left the bar after promising the bartender that he lived within walking distance. He stumbled back to his apartment where he saw a man in a suit holding an envelope in his hand waiting at the door. Men in suits hadn't been good to him lately so he assumed it was more bad news.

"Great. What now?" Fran slurred to himself.

"Are you Francisco Rivera?" the man asked.

Fran nodded.

"I'm with the law offices of--"

"If you work for that racist asshole Frank Archer, can you just leave the envelope and just go?" Fran buried his face in his hands.

"Mr. Rivera. I represent your grandmother's estate. She left you something in her will. It will have to go through probate court before it's official, but I thought you'd want to know."

"What did she leave me?"

"Her house. The nice little house by those woods."

5

Fran felt disgusted with himself that he counted himself lucky that he could get out of his lease a mere two months after he'd inherited his grandmother's house. He tried to get out of his apartment right away since he could barely afford to pay rent, utilities, and student loan payments even with his job. Without it, taking care of all of it would be impossible. He thought about how much he hated the job and how much he needed it. He felt like a parasite when he considered the timing of his grandmother's death and how if she didn't leave the house to him, he'd be moving back in with his parents.

He sold most of his grandmother's trinkets and appliances, which gave him a financial cushion that would get him through the next few months and into the summer, but by then, he'd definitely need a plan for a different job in a different field. His former boss had tons of connections, and after the way things his boss had set him up, Fran wasn't welcome at other companies in the area. Fran thought about moving to another state, but he couldn't bring himself to uproot his whole life when it didn't guarantee that he'd get the new beginning he'd be moving to find. He told himself that if he had the balls to start his life over somewhere else, he would've had the balls to stand up to Mr. Archer before getting fired. Thinking about his years of turning the other cheek, even when he shouldn't have made him look back on his life and wonder when he became that way. He looked to the horizon of his future and wondered where the point of no return was.

The floor space, formerly filled with a lifetime of clutter had been transformed into a blank canvas, save for the few pieces of furniture and appliances Fran brought from his apartment. He broke the frame of his bed when he tried to take it apart, so his mattress lay on the floor in what used to be the spare bedroom. He felt uncomfortable trying to sleep in what used to be the master bedroom since that's where his grandmother died, so that room became the designated storage room for his grandmother's clothes, papers, and other small items that weren't left to anyone else and couldn't be sold online. He kept the door locked shut and considered putting a cabinet or a bookshelf in front of the door at the end of the hall.

Nobody paid much attention to the backyard of the house in the past few years, and it had grown thick with foliage. Fran decided that he'd spend a few hours every morning clearing out the overgrown yard. That way he wouldn't sleep until noon and end up staying up all night as a result. He also figured that while so many things in his life were out of his control lately, clearing out the weeds from the yard was something he could control, and slowly improve.

On one such day, Fran heard a familiar voice calling out to him early in the morning as he cut away weeds that had ensnared a section of a fence going around what used to be an herb garden.

"Fran? Is that you?" The voice sounded familiar, but lower and rougher than he remembered.

Fran turned around to see Jack standing with one hand on his hip and the other shielding his eyes from the sun. "Jack? I haven't seen you since I was fifteen."

"Makes sense. That's when I went off to college. What are you up to these days?" Jack looked exactly the same, except six inches taller and muscular with the five-o clock shadow of an action hero.

"Want to come in for a minute?"

Fran filled Jack in on losing his grandmother and his job on the same day and how he was clearing out the yard as a way to keep himself busy while he looked for a job that would let him keep the house he inherited.

Jack furrowed his eyebrows and let out an exasperated sigh. "I can't believe that guys like your old boss can get away with stuff like that."

"It happens more often than most people think." Fran exhaled.

"Guess I haven't had to deal with it, being a white guy who got to take over the family construction business. I know it doesn't make up for what you've been going through, but I feel like I need to say it. I'll never be that kind of boss."

"You're running the company now?" Fran asked, a little embarrassed that he'd been so wrapped up in his own misfortunes that he didn't even ask about what had been going on in Jack's life.

"Yeah...Don't worry. Dad's fine. He just wants to gradually hand over the company to me as he gets ready to move down to the shore and retire. We're at the point where I basically run things. He just comes by the office to walk me through the paperwork and show up to the more important meetings." Jack pulled a few antacid tablets out of his shirt pocket and chewed them, as he often did when he was stressed.

Fran forced a smile. It wasn't that he wasn't happy for Jack. He just had to push his own struggles out of his mind long enough to smile. "That's great Jack. Your dad's construction business has been in town for so long. I'm happy for you that you're going to be running it now."

Jack stood up and looked around Fran's kitchen. "Yeah, it's my family's legacy. I guess I always figured I'd end up running the place. That's why I studied business management when I went away to college. It was either me or my little brother, and he's just not the type of guy for that sort of thing." Jack changed the subject, always trying to avoid going into detail about his drug-addicted younger brother. The Catcher family tried to hide Brad's troubles as much as they could at first, and by the time it became obvious, Jack was away at college and Fran had stopped visiting them. "Hey. Did you know that my family's company actually built this house?"

"I mean, I assumed so. From what I remember growing up around here, it seems like every house in the neighborhood was built by your family's company."

"Well...not every house. But you're probably not far off."

"Must be nice to have that kind of family history backing you up," Fran said, trying not to sound like he was bemoaning Jack being born into a family of means. Jack had always been the kid with an extra ten bucks in his pocket when he and the guys needed something, but he never once acted like he was better than anyone because of it.

Jack looked at the ground as if his thoughts had spilled out of his head and he had to read them off the kitchen floor. He almost looked like he felt guilty. "You're right. I was born into a lot of privilege, and I should really use that to help out as much as I can."

Fran nodded. "If everyone thought that way and helped out the people who really need it, I bet hardly anyone would need all that help after a while."

"Have you heard of the Oak Circle Estates development?" Jack asked, then continued. "That old forest across the street from the house here is going to have some roads cut through it and there's going to be a little suburb right where we used to hang out when we were kids. Well...we got the contract to clear the land and build all the houses."

"That's great, Jack. Though I'd be surprised if you guys didn't get the job. It's your neighborhood after all."

"What I'm trying to say is...I know that you got this great house in the worst way I can imagine, and to lose your job the same day. I can't imagine the bills and taxes piling up without a job to support the house. It would've broken me, but here you are, clearing the yard and making it better. I know I can't make up for what's happened to you, but I want to try to help. Will you come and work on one of the crews clearing the forest and building the houses?" Jack paused with an uncertainty that Fran had never seen before. It was as if Jack felt guilty for being in a position to help him. "I know it's not your field, but I'll put you on a crew run by a guy who's worked with my family for a long time, and he'll get you up to speed. By the time this project is over, you'll have enough experience to keep working in construction."

"Sounds a little too good to be true. Is there a catch?" Fran tried not to sound ungrateful but hadn't been feeling very trusting the past few months.

"Not a catch, so much as a favor that you can do for me while you're working. My younger brother, Brad...You know about his issues. I put him on the same crew to keep him off the streets and so my people can keep an eye on him. All I'd want is for you to keep an eye on Brad. Make sure he's showing up on time, not taking off to find his dealer, or faking an injury to get his hands on some pain pills. Can you do that?"

"I can look out for your brother. What about operating all that construction equipment though?"

"The job starts the last week of August, so we'll have some time to show you around the equipment. But also, we're spending August through November just clearing out the trees where the roads and plots of land will be, and then we'll pick back up in the spring with the actual construction. So, you won't have to worry about breaking one of the new houses until you've already had a few months of practice at it," Jack explained.

Fran and Jack spent the early months of the summer reconnecting. Jack would occasionally bring over some of the tools and equipment that he'd need to use come August and they'd clear out a section of the overgrown backyard. By the time Jack's 4th of July barbecue came along, the house started to feel more like his own, and less like his grandmother's. The only time he felt like an occupant of someone else's house was when he saw the door to his grandmother's old bedroom. The bedroom was still empty and he kept the door locked.

At Jack's 4th of July barbecue, Jack introduced Fran to the guys who would be on his construction crew. Jack first introduced Fran to Brody, who would lead the crew and had worked for Jack's father for a very long time. He looked like he was at least sixty-five years old with arms that looked like they were made out of leather and gray hair cut short. He looked like he could beat up guys who were half his age and twice his size. Nobody ever told Fran if Brody was his first, or last name, but he got the impression that nobody called him anything but Brody.

Jack's brother Brad reintroduced himself since he hadn't seen Fran in years. He had a wiry physique and shaggy hair. He had the words, "born free" tattooed across his knuckles. It looked like he had more tattoos, but the jean jacket he always wore blocked them from view.

Charlie Williams still lived in town and would be part of the crew. His blonde hair, always combed to the side had been shaved away, Fran guessed that Charlie had started to go bald, and rather than watch his hair slowly leave him, he decided to shave it off and make it look like it was his choice. Despite having aged noticeably, Charlie still had the same juvenile and sometimes cruel sense of humor that he'd had when he was a teenager. Fran reminded himself not to fall for any pranks that Charlie might plan.

Standing next to Charlie was Andy Larsen, a very tall and physically imposing man with long hair poking out from a baseball cap. He wore a plaid shirt unbuttoned with a tank top underneath and the sleeves rolled up to reveal his huge biceps. He seemed like the quietest of the group and always listened intently when Brody spoke. Fran guessed that Brody might be something of a father figure to him.

Pamela Janowski, known as PJ throughout the group, was the only woman in the crew and by her assertive nature, Fran could tell that she'd put up with a lot of crap from men in her line of work over the years. Every time Charlie cracked a joke at a woman's expense, or someone tried to give her a hard time, she either called them out on it directly or turned the joke around on them, making an even raunchier joke at their expense. She was muscular and knew it. She wore a tank top which revealed the tips of large angel wings that had been tattooed on her back and a symbol on her chest that looked like an eye with arrows pointing from either side of it, a star on top of it, and a cross on the bottom. Fran tried to look at it without making it look like he was staring at her breasts.

"Hey, Rivera! You staring at my tits?" she asserted with a directness designed to put Fran on the defensive.

"No," he stammered. "I was just looking at...I mean, I was trying to see...That's an interesting tattoo."

"It's an old symbol for protection. My grandmother used to draw it on all the doorways of her house," she explained as if she'd given dozens of people the exact same explanation. "I figure I'll need protection so these clowns don't drop a house on me."

"That's cool," Fran said. "My grandmother just prayed a lot when she felt like we needed to be protected."

"Guess it didn't work though. Jack told us how you got screwed over at your old job." PJ put a sympathetic hand on Fran's shoulder. "I know what it's like to deal with that kind of discrimination. I used to do marketing for a big toy company, but I couldn't keep going back to work knowing half my bosses wanted to screw me."

"What kind of big toys did they have at your old job?" Charlie asked with a suggestive wink.

"Not the kind you stick up your ass at night, Charlie," she deflected as the rest of the group erupted with laughter.

Brody laughed harder than the others and gave Charlie a playful punch on the arm. "She got you, kid."

Jack left the group to tend the grill and make his rounds to greet the dozens of people who came to attend his barbecue. As the hours crawled forward, Fran began to feel like part of the group. The feeling was alien to him, but he liked it. He also liked that Brody seemed to have worked hard to earn every bit of respect that the others gave him, but it didn't make him act superior to anyone in the group. He admired the way that PJ stood up for herself and didn't let it bother her when someone said something stupid. He wished he could be more like her. It surprised Fran how he liked the familiar, sometimes crude humor that Charlie seemed to throw at everyone. Charlie had thick skin and took the playful jabs as well as he gave them.

Everyone in the crew seemed to look out for Brad, knowing his history and how much Jack cared about him.

Whether it was Brody making sure that he didn't drink at the barbecue, or Andy subtly following Brad when he excused himself to go to the bathroom to make sure he wasn't going anywhere, they looked out for him. It made Fran feel more confident to know two simple facts about the crew. First, that they took care of their own. Secondly, it made him feel better to know that he wasn't the runt of the group.

6

The plan called for the creation of six streets. One that would cut through the forest going from north to south. The second street would cut across from east to west, but the streets wouldn't quite cut through all the way out of the forest. That way they could put in cul-de-sacs at the end of each street. The four remaining streets each took the form of a curved line coming from the center of the forest, where the other two streets met and curved towards the corners. The very center of the new neighborhood was the grass clearing with the giant oak tree at the center of it. The people who designed the planned community used the tree to name their project Oak Circle Estates. The circle of grass with the massive tree in the middle would work somewhat like a town green, except just for the neighborhood, and each of the six streets would connect with it. According to the planners, this design would utilize the space for the maximum number of houses, while still preserving the rustic, middle of the woods aesthetic that they hoped future buyers would pay top dollar to get.

Fran had worn his steel toed work boots that he'd been required to get for the job for weeks as he finished clearing out the backyard of the house. He did it partly to protect his feet and ankles as he worked, mostly it was to get his work clothes worn in to make himself look like less of a newbie. After all the time he'd been spending outside working on the overgrown yard and learning how to use the equipment with Jack on the weekends, his scrawny arms started to show the early signs of muscular definition. Just the same, he felt unsure of himself when he caught a glimpse of his body in the bathroom mirror after a shower. He asked himself if the muscle lines he saw were because he was skinny or because he was gaining muscle. He decided that he wouldn't be wearing a tank top in public any time soon and prepared for his first day on the job.

He decided to walk to work since the site was just across the street from his house. In the coming months, he knew he'd have to either get a ride with someone or prepare for a much longer walk as their work stretched towards the oak tree, which served as the beating heart of the forest. The thick brown leather of his boots had begun to break in and he made it to the site with relative ease. As the designated new guy, he spent his morning tossing fallen branches into a chipper which deposited the pulverized wood pulp into the bed of the truck. Brad dragged branches from where they fell to where Fran collected them to throw them into the wood chipper. Fran wondered how close of an eye he'd have to keep on Brad. He'd heard stories of drug addicts hurting themselves in order to get a prescription for Oxycodone or Codeine, but he didn't know how far that could go. Was Brad capable of sticking his hand in the wood chipper for a bottle of pills? Fran decided to watch very carefully at first, and then adjust his vigilance accordingly. He figured that half the reason Jack hired him was to have someone who owed him one watching his brother. If he let Brad get hurt, Jack may take back the lifeline he'd thrown him.

Brody led the crew with an experienced eye that gauged every situation the moment he saw it. Whether it was knowing when someone needed a break, or if a certain piece of lumber should be sold instead of chipped, Brody knew what to do. It seemed that the one thing he couldn't do was make a call on his cell phone. At first, Fran assumed it was because he was older than his parents, and even they had a hard time operating their smartphones, but when he tried to check his messages on his lunch break, he realized that he couldn't make a call either.

"What's the deal with the cell service out here?" he asked Jack as he tried for a fifth time to get a call to go through.

"Something to do with the valley blocking reception. I told the people who are on the business end of this that they better get it fixed if they want people to buy houses in the area, but that's their problem," Jack chuckled. "At least it means my workers won't be spending half their day texting their sweeties."

For most of the first day, Fran didn't do much besides throw the smaller branches into the woodchipper. During slower parts of the work day, PJ hoisted Fran up to the treetops in the cherry picker so he could saw branches from the trees they were preparing to take down. From the cherry picker, he finally saw how expansive the forest really was. When Fran was a child, it always seemed like an endless expanse of green, but logically he figured that the woods just seemed deeper than they were because of the labyrinthian paths through the thick foliage that didn't allow for a straight path to be taken through the forest, until now. When Fran stood at the road which served as the open mouth of the forest, with civilization right behind him and an expanse of green that he couldn't see the end of, he felt like he stood at the border between life as he knew it and another world, a darker, older world. Fran froze, his thoughts had left him hypnotized at the edge of the world until PJ jarred him back to reality as she slowly lowered him back down to the ground.

After that first day, Jack insisted on taking Fran out for a drink. They ended up at Knuckleheads since it was walking distance from Fran's house. The same bearded bartender with *Star Wars* themed sleeve tattoos slid each of them a happy hour menu and gestured with his chin towards the extensive tap list.

"Thanks, pal. What's your name?" Jack always made it a point to learn the name of anyone who worked for him, served him at a restaurant, or helped him out in any way.

"Rex. Good to meet you, bud." The bartender shook Jack's hand firmly and brought them their first round quickly.

Before Fran could make it half way through his first beer, Jack asked, "Did Brad do anything sketchy?"

Fran answered with a stare rather than with words.

"It's okay to tell me. You aren't doing him any favors by hiding anything, and believe me, after everything I've been through with the guy, nothing would surprise me," Jack pressed.

"All he did was throw the little branches into the chipper," Fran assured. "Don't you think I'd tell you if something was going on?"

Jack sighed. "I guess you would. I mean, Brad's a good kid. It makes you want to give him chance after chance, but after his last close call, we have to keep him clean."

"Close call?"

Jack took a long gulp of his beer, finishing off the glass and then signaling the bartender for another. "Eight months ago, Brad overdosed. Technically, he died for a minute there. My parents took it worse than anyone, including Brad. They told me to keep him clean no matter what and then they started to get ready to move down to the shore and retire. I think it's that they know that if things keep going the way they are, he's going to die, and after how close he came, they knew that it'd kill them if they were the ones to find him. So, you've got to promise me that you'll tell me if you even start to suspect that something's going on. If he does anything strange, you let me know."

"I promise." Fran raised his hands defensively.

A mere week later, Fran had to make good on his promise when half a dozen chainsaws went missing from the site, which by that point was a mile into the forest. He contacted Jack on the walkie talkie immediately and Jack made his way down to the site faster than Fran thought possible. He ordered different people from different crews to each help in their own way without letting on that he suspected Brad had stolen them in the night. The only people he shared his suspicions with were Fran, Charlie, and Brody.

"Whoever took the chainsaws probably stashed most of them somewhere. Nobody could carry half a dozen chainsaws to a pawn shop without being noticed. They're probably stashing them all somewhere and they'll sell them off one at a time. Let's fan out in different directions and see if we can find anything." Jack took Fran and searched the woods, heading west. He sent the rest of the crew off in other directions.

"Where's Brad?" Fran had to ask. Normally Jack drove him into work in the morning.

Cracks started to form in Jack's normally confident facade. "I don't know. He wasn't at the house this morning. His boots were still by the door. I guess he figured he could sneak out easier barefoot. I spent an hour this morning driving through all the places that he used to go to buy drugs. Honestly, I came here expecting to just tell you guys I'd be out for the day looking for him, but then this happened."

Fran saw an orange t-shirt first. Then Brad's blue plaid pajama pants came into view as Fran and Jack ran towards Brad, who stood perfectly still, staring up at the canopy of the forest. When they got within fifteen paces of them, they heard him mumbling to himself. Neither of them could understand what he was saying, but Fran noticed that it seemed to have a rhythmic cadence to it. Jack stepped in front of Brad and saw that his eyes were rolled back in his head and the whites of his eyes stared up at three trees with all of their lower branches cut off. Each of the trees had two chainsaws thrust into the middle of the tree about halfway up making them look like crosses made from trees and power tools.

"Brad! Are you okay?" Fran called out.

No response.

Jack grabbed his brother by the arm. As if Jack's touch conducted electricity through his body, Brad's posture stiffened and he fell onto his back. At first, he lay completely still, like an action figure left on a child's floor. Then he began foaming at the mouth as his body vibrated.

"Is he overdosing?" Fran held his hands over his face as if he could block out the ugly reality of the situation with his hands.

Jack knelt over his brother. "I don't think so. It didn't look like this before. Call an ambulance!"

Brad shot up to a seated position and let loose a thick spray of vomit that looked more like motor oil than anything that belonged in a human body. As the stream of vomit tapered off, Brad's voice returned, sounding raw and scratchy. "What the fuck is happening to me?"

Fran temporarily abandoned the task of calling an ambulance and rushed to Brad. He patted the young man on the back and kept quiet while Jack checked Brad's arms for track marks.

Brad pulled his arms back and scowled at his brother. "I'm six months clean. You know that, Jack!"

"Then what the hell are you doing out here?" Jack accused.

Brad finally took inventory of his situation. "I don't know. I guess maybe I was sleepwalking. My feet hurt."

"If you were asleep, then how did you do the thing with the chainsaws?" Jack balanced between an accusatory and a concerned tone.

"What are you talking about?" Brad asked.

Fran simply pointed to the six chainsaws, thrust into three branchless trees. Brad tilted his head and squinted his eyes as if looking more closely at the trees would correct what he was seeing and turn it into something that made sense.

"I didn't do that." Brad sounded like he was trying to convince himself as much as he was trying to convince Jack.

"Who else could have?"

"Look at those trees. All the branches have been cut off, and it's too narrow for someone to rest a ladder against without help. How could anyone have done that?"

Jack extended a hand to help his brother up. "I don't know."

He called the rest of crew on the walkie talkie to get a couple guys with ladders to come help get the chainsaws down. Jack explained that it must have been teenagers just playing a prank. He didn't believe his own lie, but didn't have a better explanation. Jack asked Brody to get the crews back to work while he and Fran took Brad to the hospital to patch up his scraped-up feet and figure out why he threw up.

Fran spent the rest of the day riding in the lumber truck with PJ, taking the trees that could be made sold to the lumber company in a neighboring town. He liked talking with PJ. She was everything he wished he could be, confident, assertive, and capable. When Brad went missing, Fran panicked and secretly hoped that he wouldn't be the one to find him. He remembered the somber looks on the paramedics faces as they gave him the bad news about his grandmother. He couldn't imagine being the one to give that type of news to Jack. PJ went straight to searching for him as if the task of finding Brad was completely on her. That was how PJ approached life, independently.

"Whoever put those chainsaws up in the trees must be a real psycho," PJ said to Fran without taking her eyes off the dirt road.

"Yeah. It's so weird that they would even think to do that." Fran agreed.

"I was thinking more about how dangerous it would've been. They'd have to be up on ladders in the middle of the night stabbing chainsaws into trees. Even with the best equipment, that's dangerous."

"Why would someone even do that?"

"That's the other thing. If they wanted to make a few bucks, they could have sold the saws, or if they wanted to slow down the job, they could have destroyed them. It just doesn't make any sense."

"None of this makes any sense," Fran concluded.

"What was happening to Brad back there? He was barefoot and he had what looked like black puke running down his shirt. I was in a sorority. I've seen all kinds of puke, but never anything like that." PJ cringed.

"I'm guessing that Brad fell off the wagon again. I hope not, but it's happened so many times before."

"You've known him and Jack for a long time, right?"

"Since we were kids," Fran confirmed.

"How did Brad get started down that path?" PJ asked with a sympathetic tilt of her head. "He seems like such a good guy."

"He is a good guy, but he's been dealing with addiction since he and his girlfriend got hit by a car when he was sixteen. She died, and he broke his legs. That's why he always wears long pants, even in the middle of summer. He hides the scars. Anyways, the doctor prescribed him with some Oxy, and he basically never stopped taking it. He took the leftover pills after it stopped hurting, then he bought them off kids at school, and it kept going like that until he finally made his way to a dealer. Once that happened, it was all over," Fran explained.

PJ got quiet after that. She felt like if she said anything after that she'd be judging Brad and she didn't want to do that.

When they returned from the lumber yard, Jack and Brad were back. Normally, Jack would have given a clearly sick employee the day off, but he wasn't going to let Brad out of his sight. Jack explained that after doing every drug test the hospital had to offer, Brad came back clean for everything but cigarettes. The nurses gave him a prescription for nausea even though he wasn't nauseous and patched up his feet. Brad wasn't barefoot anymore. He wore a battered pair of boots that must have been an old pair of Jack's.

Fran walked with Brad back towards the wood chipper so they could move it to the spot that Jack wanted it for tomorrow. "Do you remember anything about how you got out here last night?"

"I don't. I just remember staring up at the trees when you guys found me, and then the smell. It smelled like something burning. Then the next thing I knew I was on the ground."

"Something burning?"

"Yeah. Like burnt meat. It reminded me of a pig roast, gone wrong."

7

When the New England leaves started to change from their lively greens to the warm shades of red orange and brown, the Oak Circle Estates job started getting a lot more attention. Some of it was the type of attention that Jack said the people who bought the land and paid for the construction wanted. People who noticed that there would soon be a few dozen brand new homes in a beautiful and rustic neighborhood of a nice suburb in Hopeville, Massachusetts. A small, but noticeable fraction of the attention came from a group of protestors who bemoaned the fact that hundreds of trees would be cut down to make room for what they called McMansions. Mostly, the protestors confined their outrage to the internet, but occasionally a small group of them would stand at the end of the dirt road and heckle every car that drove by.

On one such morning, one of the protestors named Matt Harwood threw an egg at the windshield of Brody's truck. Brody slammed on the brakes of his truck and got out.

"I didn't work construction for almost fifty years just to have to take shit from some dumbass college dropout like you." Brody grabbed the young man by the t-shirt with his left hand and slammed a fist into his stomach with his right.

Matt held his stomach and curled into a fetal position. One of his friends tried to help him up and shouted to Brody. "He isn't a dropout, you fucking hick."

Brody got back in his truck and drove to the lot that they'd cleared and turned into a temporary parking lot. Everyone else had encountered the protestors too, and Jack decided that he had to address it. Brody listened in while wiping the egg off his windshield with the roll of paper towels he always kept under his driver's side seat.

"I know you've all seen the people out front, and maybe even heard from them online. Just know that we're doing everything we can to keep them out of the work area. Luckily, they aren't allowed to come onto the property, so they have to stay on the street outside the site. That, combined with the fact that there's no sidewalk, means that they can't stand there long. So just don't interact with them and they won't have anything to say soon enough."

Brody thought about the guy he punched and hoped it wouldn't come back to haunt him. He figured there was a good chance that nobody would say anything since they wouldn't want to admit that a senior citizen kicked their ass. He told himself that he'd tell Jack what happened, just as soon as things calmed down.

Jack went on. "I'm going to contact the local newspaper and try to get them to run an article pointing out some of the things we're doing to make this project as environmentally friendly as possible, and I'll make sure they know that we're even taking some steps to make sure the forest, as a whole, grows healthier for years to come."

"Are we really doing that?" PJ chirped.

"We are now." Jack replied, trying to sound funny. "We'll send a couple guys out to thin out some of the denser patches of forest, which will let the stronger plants grow better and it will make us look better in the public eye."

"I'm not on bush trimming duty." PJ decided to crack the joke before anyone else could.

He ended up sending Fran and Brad since they were the least experienced and neither of them were in a position to complain. Jack told them to focus on the bushy parts of the woods no more than twenty feet off the roads. The goal was to improve the parts of the forest that people buying the houses would actually see.

"So how long have you been clean?" Fran asked.

"Almost seven months." Brad smirked with a concealed pride. He didn't want to pat himself on the back too hard since he'd gotten clean at least a dozen times before, and relapsed.

"That's awesome. How long until you're cured?"

"Never. I'm an addict and I always will be," Brad explained as he hacked away at some tangled weeds. "It doesn't work that way."

Fran felt like he'd brought up a sore subject with Brad for no reason. He buried his chin in his chest and tried to avoid eye contact with Brad.

"I know it sounds defeatist when I say it like that, but my sponsor tells me to look at it the same way that people try to stay in shape. You're never finished with it. It's just part of who you are."

Fran stood straighter and tried not to feel so bad for mentioning it anymore. "That's really good that you can see it that way, Brad."

"Trust me. I don't always see it that way. It's just work." Brad changed the subject. "Are you getting used to working construction? It's got to be a big change from being a computer programmer."

"I wasn't a programmer. I was IT, but yeah. It's been a big change. I come home physically tired instead of mentally tired, which is actually kind of nice. The only thing that gets to me sometimes is that I know I wouldn't have this job if it weren't for your brother." Fran frowned. "I don't like knowing that the only reason I got to keep the house is someone's charity."

Brad stopped hacking at the brush and put a sympathetic hand on Fran's back. "Jack was happy to help you out. Our crew is like a little family. I don't want to sound like a therapist or anything, but we all help each other. I wouldn't be able to stay clean without you guys. PJ would be getting sexually harassed in a corporate office if it wasn't for us. Lots of people would have found an excuse to get rid of Brody since he's an older guy in a physically demanding job. And I know Jack wouldn't be able to run Dad's company without having a handful of people working with him that he thinks of as family."

"Gay!" Charlie teased.

"And Jack keeps Charlie on because he knows that nobody else would have him," Brad joked. "What's up, Charlie?"

"Jack's sending me around to get everyone back to the oak tree. He's got something to tell the whole group."

As they made their way back to the oak tree, Fran wondered if every job was so full of strange happenings. He didn't have enough experience to compare it to. Jack stood at the base of the gigantic oak tree with everyone who had arrived before them circling him. Apparently, he'd begun brainstorming ways to prove the protesters wrong and improve their public relations and wanted to tell everyone a few key points of his plan to share with the reporter who would be visiting the site later in the week. Everybody committed at least a few of the main points to memory, whether it was the energy efficiency of the homes that were being built, or how they worked to ensure the overall health of the whole forest.

Two days later, a local newspaper reporter in the form of Alice Ashby, a brunette reporter in her mid-thirties wearing dark jeans leading down to black boots and a lined flannel shirt with the sleeves rolled up that served to both keep her warm, and provide a working-class aesthetic that she thought would help the construction workers open up to her. Jack did most of the talking, but she also checked in with PJ and Fran. Brody avoided the cameras all morning until he whispered to Jack about his confrontation with the protester earlier in the week. Jack was angry at Brody for not telling him sooner, but couldn't afford to show it in front of a newspaper reporter. He discreetly sent Brody home for the day to protect the company and their operation from any fallout stemming from their confrontation. Jack made a mental note to himself that he would talk to Brody as soon as he could. He understood that Brody snapped at the guy who threw the egg at him, but also knew that it could lead to trouble for the company if they weren't lucky.

Alice asked, "How long have you been working in this community, Mr. Catcher?"

"Call me Jack," Jack insisted with a charismatic smirk. "Catcher Construction has been a family owned fixture of the community ever since my family helped early settlers of this town build their homes."

Alice tilted her head and took a more serious tone. "Some members of the community are bemoaning the fact that your company is removing thousands of trees from a forest that has been part of this community for just as long. How do you respond?"

Jack crossed his arms and furrowed his eyebrows as if he had to think hard to come up with just the right words to say. "A lot of people don't understand that we're also working to make the forest healthier, both so the future owners of the homes we're building can enjoy the foliage, but also because Catcher Construction cares so much about our environment." His rehearsed response landed perfectly. When he saw that he had Alice's attention, he continued. "In fact, we make sure that our employees bring reusable water bottles and coffee cups to reduce waste. I'd be happy to take you on a tour of the area and I'm confident that you won't see a single piece of litter in this beautiful forest."

The tour started and ended at the giant oak tree in the center of the forest. When they returned, Alice inquired about the history of the tree that would serve as a centerpiece in the neighborhood once the houses were built.

"A tree this size could be over five hundred years old!" Jack exclaimed. "That's why the community we're building will be called Oak Circle Estates."

Alice circled the tree and looked up at the goliath standing over the clearing. She imagined how it looked over the centuries, what it had seen. When she made it to the far side of the oak, she saw something that she didn't notice before. A symbol seemed to have been burned into the bark, like a brand on cattle in the Old West. The burn mark made the shape of a vertical line running through a circle, with two curved lines arcing upwards until they were parallel with the end of the vertical line. Two more curved lines mirrored them reaching down towards the bottom.

She reached out and touched the black mark on the tree, as if to confirm that what she saw was real. "What's this?"

Jack stood behind her as he regarded the strange shape. "That's Oak Circle Estates. It's like someone burned the plan for the streets into the tree."

"Why did you guys do that?"

"None of my guys did that," Jack replied.

8

Andy knocked on the heavy wooden door to Brody's tiny ranch style house. The house had been modest when he bought the house in his twenties, but with giant houses with four bedrooms or more cropping up all over the neighborhood, his house seemed almost comically small, lost in the suburbs. He heard feet stomping across the hardwood floor before he saw Brody's eye peeking between the shutters.

Finally, Brody opened the door for his young friend. "Come on in, kid." He grabbed two dark brown glass bottles of beer out of the refrigerator and opened them with a bottle opener in the form of a hula girl magnetically attached to the refrigerator door.

"So, what's going on? You sounded pretty worried on the phone." Andy sat down across the coffee table from Brody, in his usual spot.

"I hate to even admit this," Brody said, "but I can't stop thinking of what I did the other day. I can't sleep."

"That guy threw an egg at you and got in your face first," Andy defended.

"I just feel like he's going to come knocking on my door with a lawyer any moment. I mean, fuck. He might even be a law student himself. I don't have the money to fight anything like that. They'd take me for everything I have." The panic rose in Brody's voice. "Then that reporter shows up. I thought she was going to start interrogating me about it. When Jack sent me home, I couldn't even go back. I just drove. I ended up down in Connecticut, just sitting at a park by the shore, but I couldn't even enjoy it."

Andy considered what could possibly make his friend feel less anxiety about it. "I feel like if something was going to happen, it would have happened by now." It wasn't much, but he had to say something.

"What if they posted something online already? I wouldn't even know." Brody poured another gulp of beer down his throat.

"I guess I could try to look it up for you. Did you get the guy's name?"

"Matt Harwood," Brody answered. "I heard someone call out his name when he went down."

Andy took out his phone and looked him up on Facebook, Twitter, and Instagram. There were posts about the protest, but not about getting punched. Andy figured that this was because in order to talk about what happened, he would have to admit that he threw an egg at a senior citizen's truck. He showed Brody, reassuring his friend that none of his fears had come true.

"Do you feel better now?" Andy sat closer to Brody, trying to comfort him.

"I guess so," he said. "I just can't believe that I let something like that get under my skin. I felt like my life was over."

"Yeah," Andy said. "It's funny hearing that kind of talk coming from the guy who ran into gunfire to drag my dad to safety in Vietnam. Are lawyers scarier than machine gun fire?"

"They trained me to deal with gunfire. Nobody trains you to deal with snakes that show up with briefcases and accusations. Guys like that could eat you alive, turning everything you say into another nail in your coffin." Brody smirked, and then stood up and grabbed two more beers. "You've given me some piece of mind, kid. Let me fire up the grill and make you some steaks to thank you."

They finished two more beers each, ate steaks and Andy listened to Brody talk about how he met Andy's father in the service and became his best friend after saving his life. He loved the stories that Brody told, despite the fact that he'd heard them all a dozen times over. Andy knew he would always value the man who meant so much to his father, the guy who went from being a stranger in bootcamp, to the best man at his wedding, and finally the last one to see him alive, the night of his heart attack.

Brody saw Andy as both the son he never had, and the legacy of his best friend. He continued looking out for Andy throughout his schooling and even got him the job working for Catcher Construction. The two seemed like an unlikely pair, but they had become best friends, and Brody hoped they would be for as long as he lived.

"Did they take the bait, Ashby?" Alice's editor, Daniels asked in his typical gravelly no-nonsense tone. She hated when she called her by her last name, but with possible layoffs coming, she decided to choose her battles carefully.

"Nobody got defensive or made fools of themselves if that's what you're asking," Alice replied, concealing how tired of her editor's delusion that they'd be able to get some fast paced, hard hitting news into the pages of the Hopeville newspaper.

"So, what's your angle and will it be ready in time for this week's edition?" he demanded.

Alice thought about it. He'd sent her there to find dirt on the construction workers to write a story that social justice warriors could sink their teeth into and share online. Daniels was always looking for a way to have his newspaper reach far beyond the small town it served. Instead of a backwards thinking bunch of blue-collar workers, she found an interesting story about a family owned company run by a charismatic man with a good sense of how to talk to the media.

"I have an idea," Alice prompted.

Daniels looked at her over the top of his black rimmed glasses. He gestured with his hand, telling her to continue her thought.

"How about I write a piece about Catcher Construction. It's been a family owned business in town forever and they seem to genuinely want what's best for the town. The guy who is running the company, Jack, is easy on the eyes and really charismatic and knows how to charm readers with just the right talking points. If we do a piece about the town, we could definitely get local television to take interest."

Daniels held his stylishly groomed beard as if he was thinking hard about whether her idea had merit. Alice already knew that he'd go along with the story based on how she pitched it to him. She'd been working at *The Weekly Observer* for eight years and in the five since Daniels had been running things, she'd figured out his quirks and preferences.

"I'll give you a couple weeks to work something out. Don't let your other responsibilities go though. We don't have the resources for you to take all the time you need on some puff piece." Daniels always felt the need to add a hint of a reprimand to such statements.

"Thanks, boss." Alice rushed to her desk, excited to write the piece her way. She decided that she'd spend her afternoon doing some digging to get background information about the company, their employees, and the forest where they were working.

She started by going to the park and meeting with an old man named Walter, whom she knew from her days as a waitress at the local diner. Walter was over eighty years old and lived in town his entire life, which is why Alice always met with him when she needed a quote or two about local history. She always brought him a cup of decaf coffee and a glazed donut when they met.

"So, Walter, what can you tell me about Catcher Construction from the old days?" She handed him his coffee and opened a recording app on her phone.

"They've been around for a really long time. I actually worked for them for a little while, but then again, most of the young guys in town did."

"How did they treat their employees back then?" Alice prompted, hoping that he'd give more details that she could use.

"Johnny Catcher ran the company back then. He liked hiring local guys, and they worked all over Massachusetts, but he really took pride in doing jobs here in Hopeville. He was good to us, especially the local guys," Walter explained, with nostalgia dripping from his words.

"Johnny Catcher sounds like a good guy. I'm guessing that's Jack Catcher's grandfather." Alice commented before continuing her interview. "How do you feel about them cutting through the forest to put Oak Circle Estates there?"

"Doesn't really affect me." Walter shrugged. "I can't go out into those woods anymore."

Alice saw an opening. "You're saying you used to go into the woods? Did you go hiking or something?"

"A few of us would go hunting there. That's where I shot my first buck."

"Was it a popular hunting spot?"

"No. Not really. Most people didn't go there because of the old stories, but that worked out perfect for my friends and me since we were usually the only ones there."

Alice tilted her head inquisitively. "What old stories?"

"Just old ghost stories. Stories about witches back before Salem, and tales of people seeing phantom wolves or shadows in the dark. Kids told the stories to scare each other, and I'm sure each time they got told, the stories got bigger and more far-fetched." Walter sighed. "I never put much stock in stories. I've been hunting in those woods dozens of times and I never saw anything. Some people used to say that just being out there can fill you with dread, but the only feeling I got when I hunted out there was hunger. Just thinking about my days out there makes me crave a nice rare venison steak."

She walked one more lap around the pond at the park with Walter and then crossed the street so she could use the Wi-Fi at the public library. She wanted to verify as many of the details she'd just heard as possible. There wasn't much to find. The town of Hopeville, Massachusetts was a tiny village during the years of witch hunts and the historical records were sparse. After a few hours, Alice decided to make note of the old stories Walter told her about, but not to actively chase old ghost stories.

Over the next few days, she'd compiled a list of the different buildings and projects in town that Catcher Construction had built over the decades. The long list gave the impression that Hopeville wouldn't exist if it weren't for the Catcher family. Of course, Alice knew that was a silly thought. If they didn't take the jobs, some other company would have, but at the same time, the information cemented the angle of her article, painting a picture of Catcher Construction as a fixture in the community.

As Alice lay in bed next to her husband, unable to sleep, she worried that her puff piece had no teeth and seemed more like an advertisement than news. After two hours of staring at the ceiling, she decided that she would use the good press she'd given the Oak Circle Estates project as a way to land an interview with the people behind it and see if she could use her reporting to advocate for affordable housing in new developments, rather than McMansions specifically designed for the upper middle class. After having reassured herself that she could do some good in the world, she finally drifted off to sleep.

The following Saturday, Alice stopped by a local coffee shop on her way home from Saturday morning Shabbat at her local synagogue. Her husband and two kids waited in the car while she picked up her coffee and a few pastries for them, as was their Saturday morning tradition. The line was long, but Alice always preferred going to a family owned coffee shop since her money would go to something wholesome, such as a teenage daughter's college fund. While waiting in line, she saw Fran and recognized him from the interviews she did at Oak Circle Estates the previous week. She made eye contact with him and waved.

Fran approached her, testing out his slowly growing confidence. "Hey. You're that reporter that came to the site last week. Right?"

"That's me. Alice Ashby. Nice to meet you." Alice blushed. She never expected to be recognized as a newspaper reporter, but on the rare occasion that it happened it filled her with a strange blend of shyness and pride.

"Fran Rivera. I'm the new guy at Catcher Construction." He shook her hand awkwardly, only gripping her forefingers rather than her whole palm. He smiled. "I liked the article. It seemed kind of short considering how long you spent there, but I really did like it."

Alice replied, "My editor wants me to write a follow-up piece. Any juicy details I might want to know?"

"Jack's a good guy, and he treats the people who work for him like family." Fran went on and explained the way he ended up working for Catcher Construction. From their days as neighborhood kids together, to the way that Jack helped him get back on his feet after losing his job. Alice tried to press Fran for details about the company that had unjustly fired him, but he told her that he was lucky to have another job working with people who respected him and that he'd rather just move on. Over the course of their conversation, Fran tried to make Jack sound like a good person, which wasn't hard. Fran always admired Jack. Even when he teased him as a kid, he always did it the way Fran imagined a big brother would. He thought back to a time when Jack found him crying outside the local elementary school playground because an older kid stole his walkie-talkie. He remembered how Jack jumped into action and climbed the fence with one graceful motion and made the older kids give it back. He didn't even have to fight them. He just made it clear that he would fight for his friend if he had to. Ever since then, Fran felt like everything would be alright as long as Jack was around.

"I bet you're happy for your old friend," Alice prompted. "Doing all of the construction for a big project like this has got to be good for business."

Fran thought about the project and about the challenges that came with it. Between Brad's episode, the missing chainsaws, and the protestors out front, it seemed like more trouble than his old friend deserved. "Yeah. It's good for business. I just hope all the strange stuff that's been going on stops and we can just focus on the work."

"What kind of strange stuff?"

Fran realized that he'd said too much and that Jack didn't want any attention brought to the protestors, the vandalism, or his troubled brother. "Nothing. What do I know? It's my first job with the company." Fran left quickly, leaving behind both his coffee and Alice's piqued curiosity.

9

A week passed and Alice released her article. As far as Fran saw, it had two positive effects on Oak Circle Estates. First, the protesters stopped showing up after the article put the public on Catcher Construction's side. Second, Alice must have convinced the real estate company financing the project to commit to making a certain portion of the houses nice and affordable. Of course, the article made it seem like it was the company's idea all along, but Fran liked to think that Alice funneled the goodwill of her article into making a difference for the half dozen families who wouldn't otherwise be able to afford a house in that neighborhood.

While the protesters may have stopped, the strange vandalism, misplacement of equipment, and damage to the property continued. It always happened at night. That, along with some of the crews falling behind schedule, prompted Jack to assign one crew per week to work nights. He reasoned that having people on site around the clock would make it more difficult for whoever was messing with their gear to do so.

"Best case scenario," Jack explained. "It makes them stop altogether. If not, maybe we can catch them in the act. I know that you all have lives and families, so we're not going to start this for another week."

Jack was always the type of leader who wouldn't ask anyone to do something he wasn't willing to do himself, so he told everyone that he'd be spending the first week with the crew who would be manning the site, and that he'd stay every Monday with each group that followed. He knew that he was signing himself up for one sleepless night a week for the next few months, but he needed to maintain the confidence of his employees and his employers.

The first group to spend a week working nights consisted of Brody, Fran, PJ, Charlie, Andy, and Jack.

"You trying to kill us, Jack?" Charlie complained.

"Come on, Charlie. If this crew won't deal with it, how do you expect any of the others to?" Jack pleaded.

Brody chimed in. "Don't be a wimp, Charlie. We're putting in a few extra hours, but we'll be making time and a half. You don't see Andy complaining. Right, Andy?" Brody often spoke for Andy, but Andy never seemed to mind.

"Yeah. I don't mind. It'll give me time to do stuff during the day." Andy echoed Brody's reasoning.

"Yeah? And when are you going to sleep?" Charlie grumbled.

"Don't worry, Charlie. I'm sure there's gay bars open during the day too." PJ jabbed.

"Fran wishes." Charlie chirped back, feeling the need to redirect the joke onto someone else.

"Why would I want you to go to gay bars during the day?" Fran replied, using logic to make Charlie realize how foolish he sounded.

Jack decided that they'd had enough time to joke around and cut in. "That's enough. Charlie, you'll get used to it just like you did when we had to do all the night work on the highway two years back. You bitched about it then, but we got it done. This will be no different."

Fran spent the following week slowly trying to get used to the idea of essentially being nocturnal for a week. He started trying to stay up later and sleep in longer. He found the hours between two and four in the morning the hardest. The houses seemed bigger and lonelier in the silence of the late night. At times like that, he didn't have anyone to call, didn't have anywhere to go, and he got lost in his thoughts. The night left him alone with the memories that he'd rather forget, like the way his old boss treated him, and how long he put up with it. He thought about how even when he got fired, he couldn't do anything about it. He never liberated himself from the situation, he got thrown out. Discarded like the trash Mr. Archer saw him as. He thought about how fortunate he'd been to reconnect with Jack and get a job working for him, but even that good fortune had been tainted by the fact that, were it not for someone else's kindness, he'd have lost the house by now. Even the house had only come into his possession by the fact that his grandmother left it to him instead of his parents who'd moved to California when he was at college. In the solitary confinement that he experienced during those late nights, he realized that life was happening to him. He wasn't making it happen for himself. Fran decided that after this job, he'd make a big change. He didn't know what, but he knew that he would be the one causing it.

Jack invited the group to close out Knuckleheads the Friday that kicked off the weekend before they'd begin their week of night shifts. He decided that buying a couple rounds of drinks would go a long way in setting this new initiative on the right foot.

"Here's to late nights and getting the folks who hired us off our backs." Jack raised his glass.

"You mean getting them off *your* back." Andy joked. "I've never seen any of these big shots."

"Kid, that's because nobody wants you in the room when people that matter show up." Brody playfully punched Andy on the shoulder.

"That's just the way I like it." Andy smirked. "I'd rather take the late nights and the hard work with you guys than waste away in an office somewhere."

PJ chimed in. "You aren't missing much. Just imagine a maze of cubicles filled with guys who will sexually harass anything in a pencil skirt."

"See? That's how I can navigate both worlds. I can wear a tie and a hard hat in the same day, and I don't own a single pencil skirt," Jack joked.

"Fuck pencil skirts!" PJ raised her glass and the others joined her as they downed the shot of an apple flavored whiskey that their bartender Rex recommended.

The hours passed and each of them found their niche in the bar. Charlie and Andy worked their way into a circle of young women on a girl's night out and each of them tried to wingman for the other. Brody buddied up with the red-bearded bouncer, talking about motorcycles. Rex noticed Jack's Liverpool tattoo and they started talking about soccer, and traveling the UK. Rex had just returned from a three-week stay in Ireland and Jack wanted to hear every detail. Fran followed Brad and PJ when they went out back to smoke cigarettes even though he didn't smoke. He liked going with them because he liked having an excuse to step outside, breathe in the cool autumn air and talk with them. Fran had always been a bit of a loner, but he found his recent sense of belonging just as intoxicating as any whiskey could ever be.

When they came inside for another round, Jack was laughing and pounding his palm on the bar. "Guys! Check this out. Rex's entire left arm is all *Star Wars* tattoos."

Rex rolled up his sleeve to reveal a mural dedicated to a galaxy far far away. "That's right. Here's my commitment to virginity right here."

"I don't know." PJ winked. "I think they're kind of sexy."

Jack grinned and glanced at Fran with a look that said, "What's going to happen now?"

"Oh yeah." Rex smirked. "Nothing says 'fuck me' like Han Solo shooting first."

"I have no idea what any of that means." PJ giggled. She did, of course, but she also knew that a statement such as that would get under any fan's skin, which is just what she wanted.

"Jesus. I'm going to have to take you home just to make sure you watch *A New Hope* first." Rex feigned frustration.

"Come find me at last call and I might just take you up on that nerd culture crash course." PJ playfully sipped the straw in her whiskey cranberry and went to the back of the bar to start a game of pool.

By last call, Fran had lost several games of pool to Jack and Brody, Andy and Charlie had struck out with the girls, and PJ and Brad smoked half a pack of cigarettes on the back patio.

Rex announced, "Alright you drunken bastards. If you're planning on getting her number, better ask now. It's last call."

PJ closed out her tab and asked, "You going to take me to that open-all-night diner so you can explain to me why I have to start with episode four instead of episode one?"

"Anything to prevent you from making that fatal fucking error," he replied as he draped an arm over her shoulder.

When everyone made it out to the parking lot, Jack raised his arms as if to get everyone's attention. "Guys? I just wanted to say thanks for sticking by me. You guys are like family to me. I'll see you Monday night."

Fran stumbled home, thankful that he lived walking distance from the bar. He entered the house and put some leftover pizza in the microwave. He dragged himself down the hall towards the bathroom and stopped when he saw the door to his grandmother's bedroom. The door that had been locked for nearly six months. His mind whirled around the fact that he still felt like it was her house, and not his. He convinced himself that the night he opened that door and slept in the master bedroom, then the house would truly be his.

"I'm going to open that door someday," Fran promised himself before the chime of the microwave going off brought him back to less personal thoughts.

He shoveled the two slices of pizza into his mouth and fell asleep on the couch with the television on. Fran woke up with a headache, but without an ounce of regret. He was beginning to feel like humans were pack animals and that he finally belonged with a group of them. He'd take the headaches, the sore muscles, the bumps and bruises if it meant he could belong.

Monday night came and they all met at the oak tree and set to work on the house at the end of the street in the northwest corner of Oak Circle Estates. They'd just begun the framing of what would eventually become a five-bedroom colonial with a view that would look over the rest of the houses on the street the way a monarch would look over a royal court from his throne. Jack split the crew into two groups, one consisting of Fran, PJ, and Brad. Charlie, Brody, and Andy made up the other group. He'd float between the two groups and help out where he felt he was needed most.

"Remember. Cell service is bad here because we're in a valley with heavy tree cover. I'm going to go check the other side of the site. If you need me, use the walkie." Jack tried to make it sound like he was just going for a casual stroll around the site rather than venturing out in the dark looking for vandals.

Jack also planned to patrol the other streets that made up Oak Circle Estates hoping to discourage whoever had been messing with their equipment. He didn't want anyone else going on these patrols though. The possibility of Brody knocking out some teenager who thinks he was just pulling a prank, or a group of guys beating up Fran for catching them in the act made his stress-induced heartburn return. Jack swallowed some antacids and began his rounds.

He walked down the dark path, keeping the edge of the road at his side and turning his Maglite on for a few seconds and turning it off for a few seconds. At first, he did it thinking that he'd be able to surprise any vandals whom he came across if they didn't see him coming, but by the time he realized that a blinking light was even easier to see than one that was constantly shining, he'd continued to flash the light on and off simply out of habit. When he flashed the lights, he saw the door to the trailer that had been his temporary office hanging open, moving back and forth in the wind. He left the beam of the flashlight on and stepped inside, careful not to make any noise. There were little wooden dolls that looked like they belonged in another century arranged in a circle on his desk with a pile of his papers crumpled up and placed in the center of an octagon made from twigs burning in the center. Everything that had been on the surface of the desk had been swept onto the floor and destroyed, including the telephone, which looked as if it had been stomped into oblivion.

The filing cabinets were tipped over and there were several long holes punched in their metal sides. Jack couldn't tell what made the holes until he saw an axe protruding from the floor. He examined it. The axe didn't look like anything they had on the site. It had a weathered wooden handle and a rusty blade that looked like it had seen a lifetime of work. Jack held the large flashlight higher, readying himself to use it as a weapon if he had to, but he searched the small office and found that he was alone. He'd have called the police right then and there, but the phone had been smashed, so he would have to take the truck and go out to where he had cell reception to make the call. He felt that before he could go, he had to tell the others to watch their backs while he was gone, and he wanted to do it without drawing too much attention to where they were, just in case the vandals did mean them harm. That meant, he had to walk back to them.

Jack walked a few hundred paces past the area where they all parked their cars when his truck's lights turned on for two quick flashes, and then nothing. The shadow that the first flash cast made his human silhouette look like it had the large antlers of a buck coming from the top of his head. Despite the fact that he hadn't moved, the shadow cast during the second flash of light had no such ornamentation. He turned around and shined his light at the truck. The truck's high beams turned on and shined brightly at him, making it impossible for him to see if anyone was in front of him. He called Brody on the walkie-talkie and told him to bring a crowbar and approach silently from the opposite direction. Jack hoped he could handle the situation himself, but knowing that a marine who fought in Vietnam had his back made him feel a lot safer.

As Jack got closer, he sidestepped a few paces to try to get out of the beam of the light. When he did, he saw what looked like a skinny figure in a black hoodie hunched over, standing next to the truck and looking down at whatever might be in the center console. The bony figure and the black hoodie reminded him of Brad's dealer, whom he reported to the police. Suddenly, the bizarre vandalism made sense. Was it just some drug dealer's strange form of payback?

Just as that question registered in Jack's mind, Brody arrived and shouted, "What the hell is that?"

Reacting to his loud call, the figure stood up and then kept standing up when Jack thought that it had already reached its full height. The branches that drooped down and tickled the top of his truck turned out to be gigantic antlers that made the seven-foot-tall, impossibly skinny beast look even taller. Jack realized that he hadn't seen a black hoodie. He'd seen the dark leathery flesh of the beast, somehow blacker than the surrounding darkness and reflecting the light of Jack's flashlight, indicating a moist and grotesque texture to its hide. The creature glared at Brody and then back at Jack. It locked its black shark eyes with Jack's blue eyes and it charged at him with the ferocity of a wild boar.

Just as the antlers would have gored Jack, he fell onto his back and the creature burst into a thick smoke, the same dark shade of its hide and blew past him, in the direction of the road back to town.

Brody knelt down beside Jack and hoisted him halfway up by one arm. "What was that?"

"I don't know!"

"What do we do?"

"I don't know!"

The two men climbed into Jack's truck and took off down the road towards the house that the others were framing. They only made it a few hundred feet before a woman's arm reached from the roof of the truck, in through the window and grabbed the steering wheel, pulling it sharply to the left. Brody grabbed her wrist, attempting to pull her hand back to the center. When he did, her forearm ignited in flames that burnt his hand and despite her crisping flesh she pulled even harder on the steering wheel.

Jack used every ounce of upper body strength he had to keep the truck on the road, but when a second set of hands shattered through the back window and gripped bloody fingertips around his throat, he didn't stand a chance. The truck sped towards a tree. Jack slammed on the brakes, but it was too late. The airbags deployed, which saved the two men from crashing through the windshield, but the powerful airbag knocked Jack unconscious and broke Brody's nose.

Brody looked around the cab of the truck with blurry vision and saw Jack with his head tilted back, not moving. The persistent blaring horn took the pounding in his skull and multiplied it tenfold. He rolled out of the cab and onto the mossy ground and scrambled away from the wreck towards the edge of the trees on the opposite side of the dirt road. He looked back to see the tall antlered creature, blacker than the darkness with inhumanly long, clawed fingers pointing to him from behind the truck. The arms that had reached through the windows of the truck belonged to pale skinned women, in tattered clothing that looked like it belonged in another century. The women crawled like spiders into the cab of the truck and tried to drag Jack out. The huge creature picked one of them up by the ankle and threw her against a tree with force that would have shattered the bones of anyone, yet the woman scurried away with the same spider-like movement and disappeared behind the tree. Two other women, including the one who had caught fire and now looked like bad barbeque fell from the truck when the creature pulled a branch out of the tree and down onto the roof of the car, smashing a deep dent into the truck. Brody pictured a pack of wolves fighting with a bear over a kill and he knew that his friend was gone. He took off into the trees. He didn't know what pursued him, but he assumed they needed to see him, and that the tree cover could save him.

Back at the house, everyone heard the engine revving and the sound of the truck smashing into the tree. Fran stood up on top of what would one day be a staircase and saw a muted orange glow of fire in the distance. The fiery glow and the shadows it cast brought back all of the memories of what he saw when he went hunting with his father, or what he'd heard that night he spent alone in the forest all those years ago. He'd pushed the memories down deeper into his mind and dismissed them as either pranks or bad dreams, but in that moment, he wasn't sure if he'd been lying to himself all those years. He thought that perhaps something had always been in the woods, waiting for him.

"I think there's a fire down by the oak tree!" Fran called down the steps to the others.

"Andy and I will go check it out. You three stay here," Charlie commanded.

"No. That's stupid. We're sticking together," PJ asserted as she put her claw hammer into her toolbelt.

Brad and Fran climbed down from the parts of the house they were framing and joined PJ, following her lead without hesitation. Charlie led the group, walking down the dark road towards the glowing orange light until the shape of Jack's crashed truck came into view. When they recognized the truck, they took off into a sprint. Charlie and Brad ran to the driver's side door of the burning vehicle and tried to open it. The mechanism to open the door had been crushed in the crash and Brad's attempt to open it despite the damage ended with a deep cut across his left palm.

Fran circled behind the truck and looked down the road toward from where it had come. He noticed the tire marks in the dirt, indicating that Jack had been driving quickly and swerving sharply for the length of the short drive. He pulled his phone out of his pocket and called for an ambulance. After a few weeks working in the woods, everyone on the crew knew that places where a cell phone would have reception were rare, but he tried nonetheless. The call rang once and then dropped. He repeated the process twice more before shoving his phone into his pocket and looking to the others to see how he could help.

Charlie took off his jacket and draped it over the bottom edge of the broken window so he could drag Jack through it without cutting him on the broken glass. He and Brad dragged Jack a safe distance from the wreck before they really got a good look at him. Charlie thought back to his days as a lifeguard at the town pool and checked his friend's pulse. His pulse was strong, but he wasn't responsive.

Charlie started doing CPR, but during the first set of compressions, Jack's eyes opened wide and he began writhing and squirming away from the group. He screamed for everyone to get away from him until he realized that his brother and friends were the ones who stood over him. When he made that realization, his eyes widened and he slowly sat up, bracing himself with his hands in the dirt.

"What happened? Where's Brody?" Andy asked with worry in his voice that seemed uncharacteristic on such a large, muscular man.

Jack tried to describe what he'd seen and how the truck crashed into the tree, but he knew that his words didn't begin to describe what had happened. Each of them reacted differently and he knew it. Fran gave him a look with wide eyed recognition, especially when he talked about the burning woman reaching out to him. Charlie, looked at him as if he were examining his old friend, clearly looking for a head injury. PJ darted her eyes around the forest, not fully convinced that what Jack described actually happened, but certain that something in the woods caused them to lose control. Andy asked where Brody went, but this time with more urgency in his voice.

"I don't know. He was in the truck when we crashed." Jack wiped blood from his forehead and looked back at the burning truck.

Andy sprung to his feet and took off towards the oak tree at the center of the forest. He made it less than five paces when he felt a small, but strong hand grab his wrist.

"Andy. Stop! I don't believe in monsters or burning women in the woods, but something made them crash. We need to stick together," PJ reasoned.

"Get your hands off of me!" Andy yanked his hand away and continued towards the oak tree.

"Should we go with him?" Fran stammered.

"We aren't going to find anyone in the dark," Jack said ominously. "And if someone finds us, we won't be able to see them coming."

PJ suggested, "We could get some of those big floodlights that we were using back at the house, and then we'll look for them."

The five of them slowly worked their way back to the house they'd been framing, each of them looking out into the dark woods that surrounded the dirt road that they walked like a tightrope, suspended from a deadly height.

Fran and PJ grabbed the Stanley spotlights that looked like yellow laser pistols, and considering the fact that they blasted nearly a thousand lumens of light up to fifty feet, it might as well have been. Charlie grabbed a Maglite flashlight, reasoning that he could use it a bludgeoning weapon if needed, in addition to the bright beam of light that it shined into the darkness.

The Catcher brothers opened the first aid kit that they always kept nearby and began tending to their wounds. Jack pinched the gash in his brother's palm shut with butterfly closures, and then he wrapped it up with gauze. After he patched up the cuts on his brow, he dug through the bottom of the first aid kit looking for some aspirin to help with the pounding headache he'd gotten when the airbag knocked him out and probably gave him a concussion. He found a pill bottle with his father's name on it. Jack instantly recognized it as a bottle of Percocet with the name scratched off. Brad had been found with similar bottles when the police picked him up over the years.

"What the hell is this?" Jack held up the pill bottle.

Brad's eyes widened, staring at the demon that had haunted him for nearly half of his life, sitting unassumingly in a little plastic bottle. "I don't know."

"I should have fucking known!" Jack scolded. "You told us you were nine months clean, and I believed it because I wanted to believe it. We always wanted to believe you, which is why you got away with throwing your life down the toilet by the time you were twenty-two."

"Jack. Those aren't mine." Brad put his hands up defensively.

"Of course, they aren't yours. You stole them from Dad," Jack accused.

Brad stepped back, almost afraid to get too close to the pill bottle. "I'm serious, Jack. I don't know how those got in there. I'm clean."

By then, Fran and PJ had positioned themselves between the brothers. Charlie stood at the edge of the street, ready to go look for his friends, but he faced back towards the others, resting the weight of the Maglite on his shoulder.

Realizing that all eyes were on him made Jack take a hard look at what he was doing. He was angry because he cared about his brother, but at the same time he felt the urge to knock his younger brother out. Afraid of his violent urge, he stepped back and sighed. "I don't know what's going on. I don't know what tried to kill us out in the woods, and I don't know if you're clean or not. The only thing I know is that I care about all of you and I want you to be safe. Brad. If you were taking these pills, I wasn't mad because you lied to us. I was mad because you were hurting yourself. I'm going to get us out of here, but first, I need to find Brody and Andy. You all need to wait here."

"Fuck that." Charlie cringed. "I'm not letting you go out there alone. Look what happened last time."

Jack regarded Charlie and knew that he wouldn't let him go alone. "Okay. Let's go." He looked back at Brad and held up the pill bottle. "I'm still not sure if I believe you, so I'm taking this with me."

As Jack and Charlie began walking back towards the center of the forest, PJ called out to them in her signature sarcastic tone. "Thanks a lot, you guys. Thanks for leaving me to play wet nurse to these two sad sacks."

Charlie took the rare opportunity to turn a joke around on PJ. "I thought two guys and one girl was just the way you liked it."

The two men pushed on towards the heart of the forest.

10

"What do we do now?" Brad wrung his hands, still reeling from his brother's latest accusation.

PJ sighed. "I'm not just going to sit here and wait for Jack and Charlie. If even half of what Jack said is true, then there's just as good a chance that they'll need our help soon enough."

Fran sat down on the steps that would one day lead to the front door of the house. "Jack said to wait right here. If we leave, then we won't be able to find each other."

PJ rolled out a set of blueprints that Jack had been looking at earlier. "Well, if we can't leave, then let's be ready for when they get back. Brad, grab some tools that we can use as weapons if there really is some kind of creature out there in the woods. Fran, go through the first aid kit to make sure we're ready to patch the guys up if anything happens to them out there."

Brad winced when he realized that PJ intentionally kept him away from the first aid kit. He knew why Jack had a hard time trusting him. He'd lied to friends and family alike in the depths of his addiction. But Brad had been clean for a month before he'd even met PJ, and she still didn't trust him not to swallow a bottle of painkillers at the very sight of it. In little moments like that, Brad knew that even if he managed to stay clean for the rest of his life, people would always treat him differently because of his past.

Just the same, he went through the tools present and tried to wrap his head around the idea of using any of them as weapons. He'd never been a fighter. Even when he would have done anything for an ounce of heroin, he never hurt anyone physically. Brad had even been beaten up by other addicts several times over the years but he never fought back. He would just raise his hands up over his face, curl into a ball, and wait for it to be over. He brought a few screwdrivers, a crowbar, a hacksaw, and a shovel, and he laid them out on the plywood floor. He called Fran and PJ over to consider what he'd picked.

Fran hefted the crowbar and decided that the metal bar with the octagonal grip was something that could have been useful when Jack was trapped in the burning truck. With that thought, he slid the small crowbar into his toolbelt next to the spotlight and stepped back to let PJ make her choice.

"I'll stick with my hammer." PJ patted the claw hammer in her toolbelt, and then paused and picked up a flathead screwdriver. "This might come in handy if we need to start one of the cars without keys."

Brad didn't think that he could actually use anything he'd picked as a weapon, but he didn't want Fran or PJ to know that, so he picked the shovel simply because it was the largest item that lay before them. "I'll take this one."

"What have you got?" PJ asked, gesturing over to the first aid kit.

"A few rolls of gauze and medical tape. I think we should each take these with us. We've also got splints, all kinds of bandages, ice packs, and burn gel. Did anyone get burned by the truck?"

PJ and Brad looked down at their own bodies as if they had to check to make sure, then they shook their heads. Fran tossed them each a roll of medical tape and some gauze, reasoning that they might need it before the night ended.

"Here's what I figured out from the blueprints. If we can get to a car, we can take the road heading south out of the woods, but if we can't, then we'll have to cut through the trees. If we do that, then we should head west towards Spruce Street since it's only a quarter mile from the back of this house to the street."

"You really want to go into the woods after hearing about what Jack saw?" Fran stared at her in disbelief.

PJ looked back with an unaffected expression. "Do you really expect me to believe that a seven-foot-tall bear monster with antlers pushed his truck off the road when he was being attacked by women who were in the woods naked and on fire?"

Fran's mouth hung open for a moment, then he replied, "When you say it like that, it sounds--"

"It sounds fucking ridiculous," PJ concluded. "He saw something. Maybe a moose smashed its antlers into the truck and he hit the tree."

"What about the women who were grabbing at him?" Brad clutched his shovel like a security blanket.

"He was knocked out cold when we found him. Did it ever occur to either of you that maybe Jack isn't thinking clearly? He's got to have a concussion at the very least."

"You're saying there's a moose in Hopeville, Massachusetts?" Fran asked doubtfully.

"It's a hell of a lot more likely than a monster."

Brody army-crawled through the forest as quickly as he could. He'd lost track of what direction he was traveling in, but he didn't care, so long as it was away from what he'd seen at the burning truck. When he lost sight of the orange glow of the fire, he stood up and started walking in the darkness, holding one hand out in front of him to push any twigs out of the way and the other hand held his broken nose. He hoped he'd reach the street before long, but he'd lost his bearings when ran off into the trees for cover against whatever he'd seen.

He cursed himself for agreeing to the job. He was seventy years old. He could have been at home, collecting his pension, but he promised Jack's father that he'd stay on until the kid got the hang of running things. At first, holding onto the job was a favor for his old friend and a way to make his upcoming retirement a little more comfortable. Brody could have survived on his pension, but not comfortably. He wouldn't be able to take those motorcycle trips that he'd looked forward to in the years leading up to his retirement, and he wouldn't have the financial cushion to keep what he had if he had a stroke of bad luck.

Then, despite the horrors he'd just seen, his mind drifted back to his confrontation with the protestors who threw an egg at his truck. He clenched his fist and grumbled to himself when he thought about punching that college kid in the stomach. Why had he done that? He was old and tired and angry, and the kid was young, privileged, and entitled. He wasn't thinking. Back when he was that age, he could get into a fight without worrying about a lawyer showing up at his house with a lawsuit that would turn him into a homeless old man in a matter of months.

He came to a small clearing, deep in the woods and saw the beam of blue moonlight piercing the darkness. Even though Brody knew that focusing on the light would make it harder for his eyes to adjust to the all-encompassing darkness, he looked up at the full moon. When he raised his head, the light of the moon became everything and the tree branches became a black frame, outlining a piece of artwork. As he walked forwards focusing on the sky, he brushed branches aside with his hands without looking, until he reached out and instead of swatting away a brittle twig, his hand brushed against something fleshy but cold, something that moved smoothly and swung back and forth when he bumped into it. He peered upward and fell onto his back when he saw the body of Matt Harwood hanging from a noose.

Brody almost didn't recognize the man. He hadn't seen him for several months, and he looked like he'd been beaten brutally by several men before being strung up in the tree. His face was swollen and his jeans were torn and covered in blood stains. Brody crept forward and saw something carved into Matt's pale chest.

Brody stepped closer and read the words out loud. "Brody McGinn did this to me." He reached out and touched Matt's cold, lifeless leg since it was all that he could reach and when he did, images of him beating the young man into an unrecognizable pulp flashed through his mind and when he confronted the possibility that he could have done it, he let out a scream of horror that could be heard for hundreds of feet.

When he realized that whatever attacked the truck could have heard him, he covered his mouth and peered out into the darkness. His eyes darted in every direction, but after looking up at the moonlight, his eyes weren't used to it anymore and he couldn't see anything. He turned around and rubbed his eyes, hoping they would adjust, until he felt long muscular arms wrap around his body from behind. He struggled, hopelessly until he heard a familiar voice call out to him.

"Brody! It's me, Andy. You're alright."

He froze at the sound of Andy's voice. "How can I be alright after seeing this?"

Andy loosened his grip. "What are you talking about?"

"Look!" Brody gestured to the tree where Matt's lifeless body hung just moments earlier, but saw nothing. There was no rope, no blood, no sign that anything but moonlight had ever inhabited the canopy of that part of the forest. "It was right there."

"What was right there?" Andy's voice registered increasing concern for his mentor and friend.

"There was a body up in that tree, covered in blood. That college kid that I..." Brody's voice trailed off realizing that what he described seemed impossible. "It'll sound like I'm going crazy."

"It can't be crazier than what Jack told us." Andy went on to describe what Jack told them after they pulled him from the wreckage of his truck. With each detail, Brody's eyes widened with recognition that he wasn't going crazy, but the forest seemed to be.

"Kid. We have to get out of here. This place is going to kill us." Brody spoke in a harsh whisper.

Andy grabbed Brody by the shoulder when he tried to run. "No. The others will be looking for us. We have to get back to them before we go anywhere." He led Brody back towards the center of the forest.

Nothing made sense to Brody as they worked their way back towards the place he'd have given anything to get away from mere minutes earlier. He couldn't make sense of the fact that he'd fought in Vietnam, but this forest in the middle of Massachusetts had been able to get under his skin. He tried to understand why he saw the body hanging in the tree, or if it had ever really been there. With his mind beginning to fray, he could do nothing but follow Andy's lead.

The first thing they saw was the white light of the well-lit parking area near the central oak tree. Then the subtler orange glow of the burning truck faded into view, along with two distinct shadows. There were the steady, and unmoving silhouettes of the trees and their branches, and moving over and among them were shadows of antlers, and long arms, and violent struggle.

All Andy saw were flames, which sent him running to his car to get one of the gallon jugs that he kept in his trunk to try to put out the fire. He ran ahead of Brody, unaware of the shapes in the smoke that only Brody noticed. By the time Andy made it to his trunk, he heard a loud thump followed by a loud wet scream that sent him running.

They approached the car and saw a pair of legs protruding from the windshield. The light blue jeans and heavy work boots were unmistakably Charlie's. Brody took off his jacket and used it to smother the flames on the hood of the car that had begun to burn Charlie's left leg. When he saw that Charlie didn't even move when he touched the charred flesh of his leg, he feared for the worst. Andy put down the jugs of water, opened the passenger side door, and looked inside. Charlie's upper body was curled and folded at an unnatural angle and shards of glass stuck up from the flesh of his quivering neck like monuments to his eternal silence. His eyes scanned down to the burnt leg and he noticed a crescent shaped chunk of flesh missing with an artery exposed, spurting blood rhythmically, despite the wound having been burned into a charred scab. Andy wasn't sure if he was alive until he saw Charlie blink.

"Charlie. You're going to be okay. We're going to get you out of here." Andy stammered, trying to reassure himself as much as Charlie.

"Stop! Don't move him." Brody ordered, rushing to Andy's side. "If you move him the wrong way, he could die."

"He might die if we leave him like that." Andy's long muscular arms still reached out for Charlie and then dropped to his sides. "What do we do?"

As if in response to his question, PJ and Fran arrived, with Jack and Brad trailing behind. She explained how they had seen movement beyond the edge of the trees and it turned out to be Jack, who explained that he and Charlie had become separated, but couldn't put into words what had happened.

"When I pressed him to say what happened, he got all catatonic," PJ explained. "Once I asked, him about what happened all he could say was this."

"The antler man came back! The antler man came back!" He stammered as his fingertips nervously scratched at the dried blood on his lower lip.

"That's impossible," Brad asserted. He didn't want the boogeyman of his adolescence to manifest in his adulthood, but by his tone of voice, anyone could tell that he believed his brother completely.

"We need an ambulance, or Charlie is going to bleed out," Brody interrupted. "I'm getting in my truck, and driving to the road where we can get a signal and call somebody. Stay with him, and I'll come back for you when they say they're on the way."

Brody stomped to his truck, and Andy shadowed him. He didn't call out to Brody, but he decided that he wouldn't let anyone go somewhere alone in the forest. Brody shined the flashlight down and covered the top of the beam of light with his cupped palm to dampen the light and not advertise his whereabouts any more than he had to in order to see where he was going. When he saw the driver's side door of his black truck, he turned off the flashlight and made the rest of his way to the car using his muscle memory and his sense of touch. When his palm pressed against the cold metal of the door, he felt for the handle and opened it.

The interior light of the truck came on and the grizzly visage of Matt Harwood stood on all fours waiting for him in the cab of the truck, blood dripping down his face from a thick crown of thorns that clung to his hairline. The blood had soaked into his beard, changing it from light brown to a deep crimson. When he spoke, his vocal chords sounded raw and shredded, as if he'd been swallowing razorblades.

"You! Brody McGinn. You will have nothing. You will be nothing."

Matt reached out an arm with slashed wrists climbing up the forearm and grabbed Brody, pulling him into the truck with him. He threw Brody down so he was laying across the seats, and Matt climbed on top of him and spoke again, coughing blood into Brody's face as he growled, "With no home, no friends, and no dignity, you'll pray for death, living under a bridge, drinking yourself to death, and when it finally comes for you, I'll be there."

Brody screamed out Matt's name as the blood dripped into his eyes and mouth. He reached under the dashboard and grabbed the 38 revolver that he'd stashed down there in case he was ever carjacked, pressed the short barrel to his temple and pulled the trigger. The bullet passed through Brody's skull and through the back of the truck before it struck Andy in the shoulder. Tiny pieces of brain and skull splattered across the upholstery and Andy fell back, gripping his shoulder in pain.

Andy dragged himself to his feet and staggered over to the truck to see his old friend's shattered skull slumped against the driver's side seat. He saw Brody's body, but he didn't see Matt or anyone else. Andy tried to push the pain into a corner of his mind and figure out exactly what he'd seen and heard. He knew for certain that he'd seen Brody get pulled into the car, but he couldn't see who or what had grabbed him. He felt convinced that he'd heard Brody call out Matt's name right before the gunshot. And although he couldn't prove it, he knew that the forest had a way to get into a person's mind. Brody saw Matt's body hanging from a tree because it was the last thing he wanted to see. Did the forest show him Matt in the car? Did it show him exactly what would fill him with dread until he put a gun to his head and pulled the trigger? Did the forest have that power over all of them?

With these thoughts running through his mind, Andy was suddenly very aware of the fact that he was alone in the center of the forest. He felt the oak tree watching him and the branches encircling him. Without quite understanding why, Andy clambered through the forest, back towards the others. When he got back to them, he finally dropped to his knees and his hand fell from his shoulder, revealing the gunshot wound.

Fran rushed to Andy and lifted his head. "What happened? Where's Brody?"

Every time Andy tried to catch his breath to tell him what had happened, he got lightheaded and surrendered to the darkness clouding the edges of his vision. PJ sat down next to them with the first aid kit and ordered Fran to get out of the way while she examined the wound with her flashlight.

"It doesn't look like the bullet hit an artery. Hold him up. The best I can do is clean it and wrap it up until we get him to an emergency room," PJ told Fran.

"Aren't we supposed to get the bullet out?" Fran asked, remembering dozens of scenes showing just that in movies and television shows throughout his life.

"We'd probably just do more damage trying to do that. This is the best we can do for now." She wrapped the wound with several layers of gauze and secured it with duct tape.

When Andy felt like he could stand, Fran hoisted him up by his good shoulder and the two slowly trudged to what would one day be the front steps of the house they were working on earlier in the night. They sat him down next to Jack and urged him to tell them what had happened to Brody.

"I don't know. I couldn't see it all, but it looked like someone dragged him into the cab of the truck and I heard him scream Matt Harwood's name before the gun went off. The bullet went out through the back of the truck and hit me." Andy winced as he gripped his shoulder.

"Who is Matt Harwood?" Brad asked, looking up from his still catatonic brother.

"He was one of the college kids protesting us cutting down the trees out here. He got into it with Brody, and Brody punched him out," Andy explained.

PJ furrowed her eyebrows. "And do you think that this Matt guy came back and killed Brody to get back at him for that?"

The expression of pain on Andy's face was immediately replaced with one of fear. "That's not what I think. What I think is crazy."

Fran knelt in front of Andy. "It doesn't matter if it sounds insane. Everything that's been going on here has been crazy, especially tonight."

"Tell us." PJ nodded, implying a promise that they wouldn't dismiss his theory, no matter how outlandish it sounded.

"I think that the forest showed him Matt. Brody had been afraid that his punching Matt out would come back to haunt him for weeks. He even had me look the guy up online to make sure he wasn't posting about it on social media. Seeing Matt in that truck was the last thing he wanted to see, and that's why I think that whatever's in the forest took that form for exactly that reason."

"What do you mean?" PJ asked.

"I think this forest is alive, and it shows us what we're afraid of because that's our weakness. Whatever is in this forest is after us, and I think it can get inside our heads."

There followed a long pause, during which each of them digested his theory and applied it to everything they'd seen in the forest.

"The antler man came back," Jack muttered to himself.

"What is the antler man?" Fran asked Brad, knowing that Jack could not answer for himself.

From the several times Brad had gone through the steps of recovery, he was used to making confessions of his horrible past, but talking about the antler man right in the forest where he'd first seen it made him feel exposed in a way that he couldn't explain. "The Indians call it the wendigo. It's some sort of spirit. I saw it when I was out here with Audrey when I was a teenager." Brad winced as he said her name, but stood up and continued. "It chased us through the forest. That's how I broke my legs, and Audrey...well, she didn't make it."

"And you're saying that this thing is what's after us?" PJ's voice rose, making her sentence into a question. "What about the women that he saw?"

Fran stood up. "I might know about that. Do you know the stories about what happened in this forest back in Pilgrim times?"

PJ tilted her head impatiently. "What are you talking about?"

"It was like the Salem Witch Trials, except the people here didn't bother holding trials, it was more like a lynching. When they found out that a bunch of the women in Hopeville were doing their rituals out in this forest, they ambushed them and burned them at the stake."

"Witches?" PJ asked doubtfully.

"That's not all. When I was a kid, I went hunting with my dad...I thought it was just a nightmare from when I passed out, but maybe it wasn't. I shot the deer, but my hands were shaking. We tracked it for hours, and when the sun started to go down, I found it on the ground, bleeding to death, and there was a woman kneeling over it. She was sucking the blood out of the wound, and then she lunged at me. That's when I passed out." Fran swallowed hard and continued. "And a few years later, Jack and Charlie tricked me into spending the night out here alone, and... that time I didn't see anything, but I heard it. It sounded like the settlers burning those women, and they called out...not just screaming, but warning them."

"Warning them? What did they say?" Andy leaned in, focusing more on Fran's words than the bullet lodged in his shoulder.

"I don't know! I was twelve, face down in the dirt, pissing my pants." Fran shoved his fists into his pockets.

PJ took in the information and tried to be practical with it. "So how does knowing that change the plan for us getting the hell out of here?"

Fran said nothing, and wondered to himself if revealing the stories from his childhood hadn't helped them at all.

"We know that they're not just people," Brad reasoned. "I guess that means they don't want what people want."

"So, we can't reason with them," PJ rationalized. "Anything else?"

Brad remembered the worst night of his life. "I don't think the antler man can leave the forest. Audrey and I made it out of the forest, and it stopped at the edge of the trees."

PJ digested the information. "So, if we make it to the street, we're safe. That's information we can use. Fran. Do you remember anything we can use?"

"I got it. I remembered what they said." Fran stood and stepped a few feet away from the others as if he were stepping on stage to give a presentation. "She said that without them, the settlers were doomed and that the spirits would feast on them." He decided to leave out the Shakespearean dialect of the words he recalled.

"What does that mean?" PJ asked, having had enough of connecting the dots herself.

Fran rolled the words over in his mind again, analyzing the meaning and applying it to what had been happening since the start of the job in the forest. "Without them...that means after they died. I think it could either mean that they were protecting the settlers from the spirits in the forest, or maybe it means that they'd be back for revenge."

"Those ideas seem like complete opposites." Andy groaned.

"I know, but they both seem plausible." Fran shrugged his shoulders. "Either way, I think the antler thing is the biggest danger."

"The antler man!" Jack shouted, breaking his monotone mumble for the first time since they found him.

As if Jack had summoned it by calling out its name, the wendigo stood up at the edge of the trees, letting itself be seen. It stood still, with its eyes locked on Jack. Fran, PJ, Brad, and Andy cowered back, some of them clutching their improvised weapons, others standing on the unfinished wooden floor of the house they'd been framing. Everyone except Jack moved back. He stood silently and walked towards the gigantic creature.

PJ darted forward and reached out to him, but Fran gripped her shoulder and pulled her back. "Jack! What the fuck are you doing?"

When Jack reached the creature, it touched his forehead as if it were baptizing him and sank into the ground of the forest, becoming one with the shadows cast on the ground. Jack turned back, making eye contact with his brother and then turning into the darkness of the forest, and wordlessly walking into the dense woods. Brad broke away from the group and chased after his brother, vowing that he wouldn't leave anyone else behind in the forest.

"Don't wait for me! You three, get out of here. I'm going after Jack." Brad ran north into the woods, chasing after his brother.

"Fuck that. I'm not going to leave them," PJ announced. "Fran. Go to the top of the stairs with one of the spotlights so we can see what's going on out there."

Fran climbed the stairs, carrying the most powerful spotlight he could find. The beam of light cut through the darkness with a white beam that illuminated whatever it touched nearly as well as daylight. He shined the light to the north, where Jack and Brad had gone. He couldn't see Brad's orange shirt or any sign of Jack. He scanned back and forth until he saw movement and focused in on it. A dozen figures, wearing long dresses, some blackened by burns shuffled through the forest, heading south towards him and the others. He quickly scanned the spotlight in an arc and saw them coming from the north, the west, and the south. The only direction that seemed to be open was the road back to the center of the forest.

"They're coming! We have to get down the road before they cut us off." Fran called out without taking his eyes off the figures in the forest.

"Who? The thing with the antlers?" Andy asked, as he grabbed a short shovel that he intended to use as a makeshift walking stick.

Fran looked over his shoulder to call down to PJ and Andy, but when he did, he saw a woman with a face covered in dirt and hair hanging loosely around her shoulders stood over him. He immediately recognized her as the woman he saw all those years ago, standing over the dying deer. Now she stood over him.

She cried out and reached for Fran, causing him to jolt backwards, falling down the unfinished, wooden stairs. He tumbled to the bottom of the steps, smashing his right shoulder into the ground and banging his left ankle against the bottom step. PJ grabbed him and dragged him to his feet, having seen the figures in the forest closing in. Fran shrugged her off so he could slowly put his left foot down to see how badly he'd hurt his ankle. He winced with pain, but managed to keep his foot on the ground. He took a step and was able to put weight on his left ankle, but just barely. He wouldn't be outrunning anyone or anything tonight.

PJ led the group, the one relatively uninjured person left. She held the clawhammer up over her head, ready to bring it down on anything that tried to prevent them from getting the hell out of the forest. Andy and Fran limped along behind her, trying to stay as close as possible. From what they'd seen, the forest did its worst when you were alone, and so they were determined to stick together. Fran turned to shine his spotlight on the path behind them every twenty paces or so. He knew that they were surrounded except for the path back to the center of the forest, and it worried him that they only had one choice of how to escape. He thought about the possibility that the ancient witches were trying to protect the early settlers from whatever malevolent spirit dwelled in these woods. Were they still trying to protect the people trying to settle there? Were they funneling them towards a means of escape or into a trap? He didn't stop to share this with the others, because if it were a trap, then they were already caught in it. Their best hope to make it through the night alive was still making it to one of the cars and speeding out of the forest.

Just as they approached Jack's burning truck, Fran turned around again to shine the light back at the path behind them. The road had become enshrouded with a thick fog that made it impossible for him to see more than twenty yards or so behind them. The shroud of fog seemed to weaken and fade as it got closer to the group. He turned off the spotlight when he realized that the light reflecting off the fog made it even harder to see and also announced their location to anything with eyes. When they arrived back at the burning truck, Fran didn't get too close. He tried not to look at it, partly because looking at Charlie's mangled body would send him over the edge into full panic, and partly because he knew that if he focused on the darkness, his eyes would adjust and he'd be able to see more clearly.

Andy and PJ approached the truck and leaned in, looking at Charlie to see if he was still breathing. At first, they weren't sure, but then Andy swore he saw Charlie blink. They promised they were sending help, and followed Fran, making their way closer to the center of the forest.

Just as they reached the end of the road, leading to the roundabout that had served as their temporary staging area and parking lot, Fran scanned his eyes back and forth one last time, looking to the right, and then to the left. When he looked to the left side of the path, he saw a tall dark shape rising up in the fog and then reaching out with arms too skinny and frail to support such a large and monstrous beast.

"Go! Go!" He shouted as he tried to move as fast as he could on his swollen ankle.

The wendigo fell forward onto all fours, its upper body emerging from the fog as it snorted and arched its bony back. It charged with a gait unlike a deer's or a human's. It looked more like a silverback gorilla charging, with its long-clawed forelimbs gripping the ground as it thrust itself forward, pushing with its gaunt, but powerful rear legs. Fran shoved Andy out of the way as it barreled past him and into PJ. The creature hooked its antlers into PJ's flannel shirt, penetrating the fabric and cutting into the flesh of her lower abdomen. The initial charge hoisted her up and then drove her down into the dirt. The antler man exhaled harshly through its long, skeletal snout, and pinned her down with a giant, but strangely human hand with its long fingers splaying across her entire chest.

PJ looked into the black sockets of darkness where the creature's eyes belonged and swung the clawhammer and the side designed to pull nails out of boards sunk deeply into the creature's throat, entering through the side and protruding through the front before stopping as the stem of the hammer hit the moist, shadowy skin that seemed all too real for a spirit. It reared up and let out a roar that sounded like a man screaming in a cavern of echoes. When its head rose, PJ's flannel shirt ripped open, revealing a bloodstained tank top.

Andy saw the hammer hit the beast and thought that if a hammer could hurt it, then Brody's pistol could be even more effective. He ran to the truck, knowing that he could save Fran and PJ if he could get there in time.

The wendigo raised a clawed hand and began to swing down towards PJ, but seemed to stop halfway through its attack. It dove over her and sunk into the shadowy earth as it hit the ground, then emerged from the base of a nearby tree and turned its attention to Fran. It stomped towards him with a bipedal gait that still looked inhuman due to its disproportionately long arms, and clawed hands reaching out as it bounded forward. Fran knew that he couldn't outrun the charging beast, so he tried to push off on his good leg and dive out of the way at the last moment. The antler man grabbed him by his swollen ankle as he was midway through his leap and slammed him down face first into the unforgiving ground.

When he got close enough to reach the truck's driver side door, Andy dropped the shovel that he'd been using as a walking stick. He opened the door and found Brody's lifeless body lying face down across the upholstery, with a quadrant of the back of the skull blasted away in a hideous exit wound. Part of him wanted to mourn his old friend, part of him wanted to scream, and part of him wanted to run, but he knew that he'd lose more friends if he didn't get the pistol out of the Brody's pale, lifeless fingers. He extended one shaking hand to grip the pistol by the short barrel and used his other hand to pry Brody's stiff fingers off of the grip, one by one. When only the ring and pinky finger remained, Brody's other hand grabbed Andy's wrist so hard it left a bruise. Andy shook the pistol out of Brody's hand, but couldn't get free of the bony hand that continued crushing his wrist. Brody's body raised itself up to a sitting position like a marionette puppet, and the soupy mess that had once been his brain oozed out of the jagged opening in the back of his skull. In an instant, Andy's mind reeled with the list of reasons what he felt and saw was impossible. For one, Brody was dead. Another impossibility was his strength. Andy had been lifting weights regularly for half of his twenty-six years and had even briefly flirted with the idea of lifting competitively, but somehow, he couldn't pull away from an old man's grip. He put his foot up against Brody's ribs so he could push back with his legs while pulling with all of his upper body strength.

After a few seconds of this struggle, Andy heard a muted popping sound and felt a sharp pain shoot up his right arm. He cried out and kicked one more time and fell back onto the ground. His right hand hung limply at the end of his arm, and he couldn't move it. Andy scooped up the pistol with his left hand, and aimed it at the cab of the truck. He waited for Brody's puppet body to slither out after him. It never did. He looked back into the cab and saw the body in the same position he'd initially found it in. Realizing that there wasn't time to consider what had just happened, he raised the pistol and aimed it at the towering creature that now stood over Fran. He fired the remaining five shots in quick succession and saw that the shots had either not affected the antler man or had missed entirely.

Determined to save his remaining friends, he pushed Brody's now still body over and got into the truck, putting it into gear and driving it straight through the malevolent spirit. The creature sank out of existence as the truck would have hit it, and the truck continued on, not even slowing down as it smashed into the burning truck and exploded in a fireball that killed both Andy and Charlie.

Fran dragged himself halfway up and looked at the harsh blaze for just long enough to register what had happened before a woman's arm reached around his throat and pulled him into the trees before shoving him down to the ground, pressing a hand over his mouth to keep him from screaming. She held a box cutter to his chest. Just as he realized that it was PJ that pulled him away and started to feel relieved, PJ pulled open his button-down shirt and began slowly cutting a curved line just beneath his collarbone. His eyes got wide and he bit down on PJ's hand until he tasted blood, but she continued slowly dragging the blade across his chest.

11

Brad bounded through the forest, going as fast as he could without tripping over a root and twisting his ankle, but despite his efforts, he couldn't seem to bridge the distance between him and his brother. After a few hundred feet of trying to catch up to Jack, his mindset shifted from trying to catch up, to just trying to keep up. Brad knew deep down that if he let Jack out of his sight, he'd never see him alive again.

Although he knew cognitively that his eyes should be adjusting to the dark of the forest, it only seemed to get darker. The idea of him running blindly into the woods that had taken so many lives, caused him to slow down but not stop. He couldn't bring himself to stop, not only because it would give his brother more time to get out of his eyeshot, but also because he felt like it would provide an opportunity for the antler man to catch up with him. Brad thought about all the times that Jack had saved him, bailed him out, or otherwise been there for him over the years and knew that he had to do everything he could to save his brother.

His thoughts were interrupted by the sensation of his head snapping backwards as his body continued forward. Brad's body tilted backwards until he was horizontal in the air and fell onto his back. Staring into the starlight, he saw the frayed and interconnected ropes that had faded from white to beige over the years. He immediately recognized the rope that close lined him as the frayed remnants of the hammock that he'd spent half a summer laying in with Audrey all those years ago. He groaned, and began to work up the willpower it would take to get up from the ground when a familiar face approached from the direction he'd come and stood over him, looking down at him.

"You look like shit, little brother." Jack smirked.

After considering the direction Jack had come from, Brad realized that he'd either outpaced his brother or Jack circled around and positioned himself behind him. He tried to get up, but Jack pressed his boot down on his shoulder, pushing him back into the dirt.

"Don't get up, Brad." Jack's voice came out smooth and confident, but with an edge to it that Jack had never heard before. "You're right where you belong."

"Quit joking around, Jack. We have to get out of here," Brad pleaded as he rolled onto his stomach and tried to push himself up onto all fours.

Jack swung his boot into Brad's ribs with a hideous cracking sound. Brad curled into a ball, clutching his stomach as he endured stomps and kicks from his older brother, the most painful of which crushed his right ankle. It would have broken if he hadn't been wearing boots, but he knew he'd be limping for weeks, if he lived that long.

"Jack...Why?" Brad groaned.

"Because when you and Audrey came out here, she should have been the one to come back. Not you. She would have had a life. You just crawled into a pill bottle and hid there for half your life." Jack circled his brother with the focus of a shark circling a seal before going in for the kill.

Brad crawled through the dirt and the rocks and the pain, trying to get away from his tormentor. He managed to grab a fallen log and grabbed at the bark with his shaking hands. He hoped he could hoist himself over the log and roll down the hill that would take him far enough away from Jack that he could crawl under a rock and hide from his brother.

Suddenly, he felt a sharp pain in each of his hands. He instinctively tried to jerk his head towards the source of the pain, but since his hands were stretched out to either side of his body outside of his peripheral vision, all he could do was look straight ahead and howl with pain.

When he screamed all the air out of his lungs, he was finally able to look at each hand at the source of his agony. A flathead screwdriver pinned his right hand to the log, and a Philips head screwdriver pinned down his left hand. Jack keeled down in front of his little brother and stood nose to nose with him.

"Did you ever think that it was your fault that the antler man came after you and Audrey? It never showed up, drooling all over her tits until it saw you fucking her in that stupid fucking hammock." Jack pressed his fingertip against Brad's forehead.

Brad had blamed himself for what had happened to Audrey for most of his life. Every time he shot up and thought that it might be the last time, he felt like he deserved it. He thought back about every sleepless night he spent picturing the antler man, and Audrey's final moments of horror. As the memories raged through his mind, Brad noticed one thing out of place. He'd never told Jack that he and Audrey were having sex when she first saw the antler man. Brad had decided to keep that part secret, as if it would have been shameful for Audrey if people knew. There was no way he could have known about the antler man standing over her, giving her the horrible vision that set off the chain of events leading to the end of her life.

Brad hesitated, then said, "You're not Jack. Jack never knew about that."

Jack stood up and looked down at the ruin of his brother. When he spoke, his voice came out deeper and with a blend of different accents that Brad couldn't identify. "That doesn't matter anymore. You may have some idea of what I am, unlike Charlie. All he could do was ask why before I pushed the glass into his throat. You may understand, but you're not going anywhere. Your spirit died in this forest years ago, and your body will follow suit."

Brad couldn't accept that his brother had killed Charlie. He looked up at his brother and saw Jack trapped behind his own eyes. Brad imagined Jack's soul locked away by whatever lived within him now. He imagined Jack's captor tearing off chunks of his soul whenever he could use it to hurt someone. He couldn't bring himself to accept that his brother was gone. "You're right. I died here. I deserve to die here. Take me, and let Jack go."

Jack leaned in and put his palms on top of each screwdriver, pressing them through Brad's hands and further into the wood of the decaying log. "Wait right here. When I'm done with your friends, I'll return, and I'll be hungry."

Brad's mind swirled with the recollection of what Audrey had told him about the wendigo representing cannibalism, and that some tribes believed that if they ever resorted to cannibalism, they'd become a wendigo. He thought back to the wound that he saw on Charlie's leg and realized that it looked like a bite mark. He retched and squinted his eyes shut tightly, fighting back the image of his brother eating human flesh, and when his eyes opened, Jack was gone.

PJ fought through the pain of Fran biting down on her hand and continued dragging the razor blade across his chest, always careful not to cut too deep. She wanted to cry out, or at least tell Fran what she was doing, but that would draw the attention of the antler man which seemed to be more focused on Andy's body, which made PJ think that maybe he wasn't dead yet. She tried not to think about her friend in the truck, spending his final moments in agony as the hellish creature preyed on him. There was nothing she could do for him, but maybe she could save Fran and herself.

The creature stopped and stood up on its hind legs, adopting a more human appearance before turning towards the tree that PJ had dragged Fran behind. It sensed them, not by scent and not by sound, but by some instinct older than humanity that led the creature to its prey. It charged towards them, feeling no need to sneak up on them. It new that neither of them was in any shape to run or fight back.

When the wendigo curled its body around the tree to attack, PJ rolled onto her back next to Fran, held up the boxcutter weakly with one hand and used her other to push the fabric of Fran's shirt to the side, making sure his fresh cuts were visible. The wendigo saw the blood beginning to pool up in the shape of the cuts on his chest, which matched the protection rune tattooed on PJ's chest exactly. It backed up, not attacking, but not retreating either. It circled them at a distance, looking for a weakness in their newfound defenses.

Staring at the nightmarish creature, Fran asked. "Why didn't it kill us?"

"I don't think it can hurt anyone who has this symbol on their skin." PJ gestured to her tattoo and then to the matching cuts on Fran's chest. "That's why I did that to you."

Fran clutched his chest in pain. "Sorry if I don't thank you for that."

"I'm sorry. I couldn't think of anything else that could protect us." PJ put her bloody hand on top of Fran's. "Let's get out of here."

"What do you think happened to Jack and Brad?" Fran groaned as PJ pulled him to his feet.

"I don't know, but we'll never find them out here like this. We'll send help when we get out." She turned and led the way back to the dirt road out of the forest.

Fran looked over his shoulder at the path behind them and saw the antler man charging them, and then turning away when Fran cried out and they turned to face the monster. PJ's eyes widened with shock, and they stopped their slow and laborious trudge.

"What the fuck was that? I thought it couldn't come after us if we have these." PJ gestured to her chest.

"It stopped when I turned to face it. Maybe it has to see the symbol for it to work." Fran suggested.

PJ turned Fran around so they stood back to back and locked arms with him. "Even if it doesn't help, we'll be able to see it coming."

The two awkwardly walked down the dirt path leading away from the center of the forest with their backs to one another to use the symbols on their chests to keep the creature away. After a few hundred feet of this strange dance, the wendigo turned and walked down the path towards the center of the forest, seemingly giving up on being able to attack them, since the symbol of protection had an effect on it. Fran expressed his relief that it seemed to be letting them go, but PJ insisted that it must have some other way of coming after them, something that could bypass their new form of protection. Soon the flames of the burning truck and the gigantic oak tree were nothing more than specks behind them.

PJ heard something ahead of them, less than one hundred yards from the road. "Wait Fran!" She called out in a harsh whisper. "There's something in the trees up ahead."

They stopped and steadied themselves. Fran held up the crowbar he had in his toolbelt, and PJ held up the boxcutter and wished she hadn't dropped the hammer when she hit the wendigo with it. The rustling in the trees continued at a steady and even pace, twigs snapped and branches swayed as whatever followed them were stalking them from just out of sight. Soon they saw Jack walking out of the trees, with blood dripping onto his face from a cut on his forehead.

PJ jogged over to him. "Jack! Are you okay? Where's Brad?"

"Those witches killed him, and ate him." Jack lied. "It was horrible."

As Jack continued telling PJ a fabricated version of what had happened since they last saw the Catcher brothers, Fran heard the voice of a child behind him. He turned and saw a little girl in a muted gray dress with a white apron in front and a dirty white bonnet covering her curly blonde hair. With everything that he'd seen in the forest, Fran knew that he should have been terrified, but something in him told him to wait and listen.

"Beware the pretender that stands before your companion. He is not who he says he is. A malevolent spirit dwells within his flesh. It feeds on his soul, and he will feed on your bodies," she warned.

"PJ! Wait!" Fran shouted.

As she turned to see why he was shouting, Jack's facade fell from his face, revealing his true murderous intent. He held up a folding knife with a four-inch blade up high and prepared to bring it down on the back of PJ's head.

12

In the split second it took for Jack to bring the knife down, PJ could only manage to turn around and raise her left hand defensively. The blade of the knife penetrated through her hand and stopped less than an inch from her eye. She pushed forward, knowing that even though it made her hand burn with agony, that it got the tip of the knife away from her face.

Fran knew that in the time it would take him to walk the twenty feet to get to them, Jack would have plenty of time to kill PJ, so he threw the crowbar and hoped for the best. It sailed through the air and the side of the crowbar's handle hit Jack in the chest. The impact would leave a bruise, but in the moment, it would do nothing to stop Jack's attack. Fran tried to shine the beam of the spotlight into Jack's eyes, but he didn't flinch. Whatever evil had taken control of Jack's body, didn't need eyes to see.

PJ slashed her razor blade down the length of Jack's calf muscle and scrambled away on all fours. As she got closer to Fran, she called out, "Go! I'll catch up."

Fran began limping towards the edge of the forest, and just like she told him to, PJ caught up to him in mere moments. She stood back to back with him, but didn't lock arms like she'd done before. She knew that the forest's new way of attacking them couldn't be stopped by the protection rune on her chest, so she needed her hands free to defend herself with the flathead screwdriver which was the only weapon she had left. She told Fran not to slow down no matter what happened. He'd need to move as quickly as he could. Jack's pursuit had been slowed down significantly because of the gash in his leg, but he could still move more quickly than Fran could with his injured ankle. They all hurried to the forest's edge as fast as their broken bodies could carry them.

PJ had a plan that she wouldn't share with Fran until the time came. She wanted to save her friend, Jack. She planned to let him follow her closely enough that she could grapple him at the last moment and throw him out of the forest, hoping that Jack leaving the woods would expel whatever evil spirit had inhabited his body. She decided not to tell Fran because she worried that he'd either talk her out of it or try to help and get himself killed. As they got within five feet of the road, PJ grabbed Fran and threw him into the road, where he landed on his stomach. He rolled over and looked back at PJ without getting up.

She rushed forward towards Jack and kicked a booted foot into his stomach. As he clutched his stomach, she grabbed the knife out of his hand and threw it out into the street. Once there were no weapons involved, she grabbed her friend by the back of his shirt and tried to drag him to the edge of the forest. Jack landed punch after punch, but she shut out the pain and kept pulling him. When they were just a few feet from the forest's edge, she heaved with all her might and he began stumbling along with her, but when she reached the border between the woods and the rest of Hopeville, she continued but he finally writhed free. She fell forward from the momentum of it and ended up on the pavement right next to Fran.

Jack's eyes pleaded for them to find a way to take him with them, to save him, but his mouth spoke in a voice that was not his own. "He doesn't belong to you anymore. He belongs to us now."

Jack's hands shook as they moved, in an internal war with his old self and the evil that had taken his body from him. He reached into his shirt pocket and pulled out a small replacement blade for the utility knife that PJ had taken away from him. His eyes widened with terror as he realized what his body intended to do to him. Jack tried to cry out, but all he could do was open his mouth as the force within him drew the blade to his throat and drew it downward opening his vein and spilling gouts of blood onto the forest floor.

PJ sprang to her feet ran back to him and dragged him out of the forest. He seemed to return to his normal self when she got him into the street, but the damage had been done. She and Fran cried out for their friend to hold on, but could do nothing. Fran pulled his phone from his pocket, sure that he'd finally have service, and he called for an ambulance to come even though he knew deep down that they'd never arrive in time to save Jack.

Fran dropped to his knees and locked eyes with his childhood friend. In the blue of his eyes he saw the charismatic young man he knew when he was just an awkward kid. He saw the guy who threw him a lifeline when he'd lost his job and his grandmother in the same day. He saw someone who would always accept him and never let him down.

Jack's eyes relaxed with acceptance and he stopped resisting. Fran watched his friend's lifeforce fade away as the hint of dawn began to crest the horizon and he heard sirens in the distance.

Brad repositioned his body, but could not pull his hands free from the log they'd been pinned to. The more he struggled to get free, the more lightheaded he felt. He tried to get free, but knew he couldn't let himself pass out. Being trapped in the forest was bad. Being unconscious and defenseless in the forest would be worse. He tried to pull the screwdriver out of his right hand with his teeth, but his vision began to blur and he stopped. His head drooped downward and he closed his eyes.

Brad took several deep breaths, and stopped when he heard a voice singing. First, he recognized the words, as a song from The Distillers. At first the words seemed out of place without the raspy melody of Brody Dalle singing it. Then he recognized the voice that he hadn't heard in over a decade. Audrey's soft voice continued humming the melody in his ear as she stepped in front of him and kneeled down.

"Are you real?" Brad tilted his head and squinted his eyes, wondering how close to death he was.

"I missed you too," she smirked. "I'm as real as the antler man, and the thing that's making Jack try to kill you."

"I'm so sorry, Audrey. I let you die here, and I wasted every day of my life since." Tears streamed down Brad's face.

"You didn't let me die. And as far as you wasting your life goes, you can't make it right if you die out here too." She reached out and grabbed each screwdriver. "Baby, I'm sorry for how this hurts, but we need to get you out of here before they come back."

She pulled the screwdrivers from the log and Brad cried out in pain. Audrey hadn't changed in all the years since he'd seen her. She still wore leggings under her black denim shorts and she still wore the t-shirt she bought at the Against Me concert.

"You know, I still have mine," he groaned.

"Still have what?" she asked as she wrapped his arm over her shoulder and took the weight off of his shattered ankle.

Brad couldn't form words. He just tapped a bloody finger against the enamel pin in the shape of a black feather that he bought at the same concert and pinned to the lapel of his jean jacket. She smiled and continued leading him north towards the edge of the forest.

"Have you always been here?" Brad slurred, just on the edge of passing out.

Audrey hesitated, knowing that couldn't lie to him, but that if she didn't choose her words carefully, it would shatter him and destroy the will that was keeping him alive. "Yeah...My spirit, or whatever, is here at night, and I can't leave. It's not as bad as it would have been if you let the antler man get me though. He has their spirits. I may be stuck here, but at least I'm a free spirit."

"You always were." Brad dropped to his knees.

"Don't stop now, baby. We're almost there," Audrey pleaded.

He looked up at the love of his life. "But if I stop now, and it doesn't get me, won't we be together?"

"I want you to live!" she exclaimed. "Find me and find a way to free me. But most of all, I want you to go and live like we planned."

He pushed himself to his feet, and staggered towards the edge of the forest. Audrey gave him one last push and he stumbled onto the asphalt and passed out on the cold ground. The sun slowly began to rise and Brad reached out towards the red flashing lights of the ambulance that passed him. The ambulance screeched to a halt and the paramedics checked his vitals before loading him up into the back and continuing to the entrance of the forest where PJ and Fran waited for them.

13

It took the paramedics mere minutes to get to the forest, and once they confirmed that Jack had died, they began treating PJ, Fran, and Brad. When the second ambulance and a police car arrived, they found the wreckage of the burning trucks quickly.

The police believed the story that PJ and Fran agreed on, knowing that they'd look crazy if they tried to tell the truth. They resolved to find a way to destroy what had taken their friends from them, and they knew they couldn't do that from the inside of a padded cell. The official story was that Jack tried to fire Brody for his violent outburst with the protestors, and when that happened, he flew into a homicidal rage that PJ, Fran, and Brad barely escaped. Their story told of Jack saving them, which would account for the injuries he'd sustained throughout the night, and saying that Brody cut Jack's throat before going back to the forest and taking his own life. It sickened them to lie about Brody, but they offered the story about him up as a sacrifice to give them the time to bring real justice to the evil spirit actually responsible for their friends' deaths.

Brad tried to tell the truth. Nobody believed it. People either distrusted him altogether because of his past as a drug addict or attributed his outlandish story to his mind blocking out the traumatic true events and replacing them with something else. As he recovered from his injuries, he eventually stopped answering questions, realizing he could only rely on himself to honor the dead and find a way to prove what had happened to them.

Jack left the construction company to PJ and Brad. Brad became the face of the company and carried on his family's traditions by faking the charisma that had come so easy to his brother during the day and spending the nights working on plans to destroy the evil spirit that took away both his brother and the love of his life.

PJ worked with Fran to incorporate the runic symbol that had saved them, along with others into the designs of the fences around the yards, the ornate guardrails that they claimed would keep deer off the roads at night, and on the doorways of each home. That way, the evil that had preyed on them could only exist in the forests beyond the edge of the property. They hoped that none of the future home owners would take them down before they thought of a way to do away with the creature that haunted the forest.

As the construction of Oak Circle Estates came to a conclusion, Brad moved into a small cabin that they'd built on a quarter acre lot that his brother had set aside for him and worked into the negotiations to do the project. He spent most of his days there alone, and Audrey would come to him at night, and the two would laugh at the irony of living in a cabin after Audrey told him that she wanted a treehouse on their last night together. While Audrey felt a reprieve from her deathly imprisonment when Brad moved into the cabin, he burned with a desire to find a way to free her spirit from its prison.

Alice Ashby wanted to visit Brad, Fran, and PJ in front of the Oak tree at the center of Oak Circle Estates, but PJ insisted that they meet in the living rooms of one of the houses that had been completed. She claimed that not only would it be more comfortable for everyone involved, but it would also give a good photo opportunity to show the inside of the houses that would be going onto the market the following week. Alice immediately noticed that PJ was a tough negotiator and she knew that she wouldn't get the interview without giving PJ a few concessions. They sat on couches on either side of a coffee table that had been set up just for the interview. Alice sat in a leather recliner that made it feel awkward for her to lean forward and take notes. She turned on the recording app on her phone after asking the three if they were okay with being recorded.

"Thanks for meeting with me," she said with an even a formal tone, suggesting that this was her first line in every interview.

"It's our pleasure," Brad said with the charm that he'd become increasingly good at faking the past few months. In fact, sometimes he wasn't even sure if he was acting or not.

"The houses look beautiful. Are you looking forward to finishing this project?" Alice smiled and stared at the three, waiting for a response.

"Thank you so much, Alice." PJ smiled, playing nice. "Finishing any big project is bittersweet. While it's exciting to see these houses ready to become homes as families move in, it will be difficult to walk away with from the project that we really poured our hearts into."

"I'm surprised to hear you say that." Alice dropped her smile, knowing that the interview could take a turn for the worse with this line of questioning.

"What makes you say that?" PJ tilted her head in frustration, giving Alice one last chance not to go there.

"With what happened to you six months ago, I suspected that you'd be happy to leave it all behind."

"Why the fuck would you bring that up?" Fran stood up from the couch and paced around the room. "Brad lost a brother, and we all lost good friends."

Alice took cover behind both her notebook and her principles as a journalist. "My first loyalty is to the truth, and sometimes the truth is uncomfortable."

Fran stopped pacing and crossed his arms. "The public knows what happened, and it's obviously not going to happen again. All you're doing is using what happened to us to try to sell a few papers. You're not serving the public. All you're doing is making us relive the trauma. It's not what we want and it's definitely not what our friends would have wanted."

"Easy, Fran," PJ interrupted. "Alice here's just trying to do her job."

Fran scowled but deep down felt proud of himself. Just a year earlier, he would never have had the confidence to stand up to someone like that. He knew that his anger was ugly, but he finally believed he could show the world how he felt. He knew that Jack set him on this path to his new, more confident way of being. Thinking about his old friend turned his anger into sorrow.

PJ, who introduced herself to Alice with her full first name, Pamela, stood up from the couch and walked to the front door of the house. "I think some fresh air would be good for us. How about I take you on a walk around Oak Circle Estates, and you can finish up with Brad when he walks you back to your car later?"

Alice sensed that it was an order more than a request, so she went out into the neighborhood with PJ, who showed her around and talked about whatever Alice wanted, giving short and not particularly juicy responses to questions about the violent incident that had occurred six months earlier and providing articulate and charming insights to questions about the company, its future, and the project. Alice sensed that there was more to that blood-soaked night, but knew that she wouldn't be able to get anything out of them until an opportunity presented itself. She decided to bide her time and wait for an opening that would give her the big story that she suspected lay beneath the surface of Oak Circle Estates.

Back in the house, Brad turned to Fran. "What the hell was that about?"

"I'm not interested in playing nice with the reporter. I'm more interested in why you haven't been coming to the house to figure out a plan to make things right again."

"Why should I? It's always the same. We can think of ways to contain it, to prevent things from happening again, but never anything to make what happened right again." Brad intentionally left out any information about the apparition of Audrey he'd seen that night in the forest, but he wanted to find a way to free her spirit from its entrapment even more than he wanted to avenge his friends and brother.

"We may not know how to fix things yet, but someday we will. Someday we'll go back into that forest ready to fight, and when that day comes, we need to be a family. We only made it through that night because we looked out for each other like a family." Fran reached out to Brad.

"My family is dead." Brad pulled away from Fran's touch.

"Your family is waiting for you, Brad. We'll be ready to fight it someday, and I hope you'll be ready to fight with us."

After work, Fran met up with PJ at his house and they walked down the long hallway to the room that had once been his grandmother's and then had been closed off for months, but now served as a room dedicated to understanding their adversary. Cork boards on the wall held notes about groups of people who might understand more about the symbols that had saved them and could help. They'd compiled a list of sightings of the wendigo and other legendary creatures that sounded similar such as the wechuge and the wind walker. A desk in the corner held all of their research about the coven of witches that had tried to protect them and warn them about the evil that waited for them in the forest. A whiteboard on the wall was covered with thoughts and ideas about what could possibly hurt a spirit.

The two readied themselves in their ongoing ritual of preparing for the day that they would understand what they were truly up against and could fight back against the insatiable spirit dwelling within the forest.

Acknowledgements

Thank you, Amanda, not just for the incredible cover art that makes this book look awesome, but also for the love, encouragement, and inspiration that you give me every day.

Thanks to Zoey, our puppy (or Dogter, as my students call her), for keeping me company when I'm writing and barking whenever anything at all happens.

I absolutely must thank Nancy Manning, a former professor of mine who noticed me writing in the back pages of my college notebooks before and after class and asked me about what I was writing for myself. She took a look, became one of the biggest supporters of my work. Your keen eye, insights, and attention to detail have been incredibly valuable.

A big thank-you to my parents, who always allowed me to be creative, and encouraged me to take a look behind the scenes of the books and movies I loved which helped me to really appreciate all of the creative people in the world and to strive to be one of them.

Thanks to Marc for being there to talk about books, fishing, music and hockey. A big thanks for all the adventures we get into which may make it into these books with names changed to protect the guilty.

Thanks to Steve for your friendship, and for letting me ask you science-related research questions for writing these books that I'd rather not have in my search history

Thanks to Gonz for being one of the most loyal and reliable friends I've ever had.

Thanks to Julie for being as excited as you were when I told you I was going to focus on writing horror.

Thanks to Karen and Belle from That Bookstore in Wethersfield, CT for being so welcoming to Amanda and I, and for running an absolutely ideal bookstore to spend an afternoon in.

And again, thanks to you, dear reader.